SPARTAN QUEST

THE FIRE OF ARES

SPARTAN QUEST

THE FIRE OF ARES

MICHAEL FORD

Walker & Company • New York

First published in Great Britain by Bloomsbury Publishing Plc
Published in the United States of America by Walker Publishing Company, Inc.
Distributed to the trade by Macmillan

For information about permission to reproduce selections from his book, write to
Permissions, Walker & Company, 175 Fifth Avenue, New York, New York 10010

Library of Congress Cataloging-in-Publication Data
Ford, Michael (Michael James).
The Fire of Ares / Michael Ford.
p.   cm.
Summary: When slaves rebel in ancient Sparta, twelve-year-old Lysander,
guarded by an heirloom amulet, the Fire of Ares, is caught between the Spartan
ruling class, with whom he has been training as a warrior since his noble heritage
was revealed, and those among whom he was recently laboring as a slave.
ISBN-13: 978-0-8027-9744-5 • ISBN-10: 0-8027-9744-X
1. Lysander, d. 395 B.C.—Juvenile fiction. [1. Lysander, d. 395 B.C.—Fiction.
2. Slavery—Fiction. 3. Amulets—Fiction. 4. Social classes—Fiction.
5. Sparta (Extinct city)—Fiction. 6. Greece—History—Spartan and Theban
supremacies, 404–362 B.C.—Fiction.] I. Title.
PZ7.F75328Fir 2008   [Fic]—dc22   2007024237

Visit Walker & Company's Web site at www.walkeryoungreaders.com

Typeset by Dorchester Typesetting Group Ltd
Printed in the U.S.A. by Quebecor World Fairfield
2 4 6 8 10 9 7 5 3 1

All papers used by Walker & Company are natural, recyclable products made
from wood grown in well-managed forests. The manufacturing processes
conform to the environmental regulations of the country of origin.

For Rebecca
With thanks to Emile Farley

PROLOGUE

Thorakis tugged back on the leather reins, and his stallion skidded to a halt on the dusty track.

'Good work, Hermes,' he said, patting the horse's jet-black flank.

Thorakis looked across at Demokrates. His younger brother sat alert in his saddle. The breeze from the Aegean Sea behind them ruffled the red plume of his bronze helmet. Above, slender wisps of cloud floated across the blue sky.

As Thorakis gazed up a solitary hawk glided past, hanging in the air.

'The priests would call that a good omen,' said his brother.

'We don't need omens,' replied Thorakis. 'I already know my destiny lies here . . .' He patted the sheathed sword at his side.

The light wind stilled, and Hermes pricked his ears. Thorakis heard it too – the noise of distant battle creeping over the brow of the hill: the clash of iron on

1

bronze, the war cries. And there was no mistaking the smell – the odours of blood, of sweat, and of men's fear.

The scent meant something else as well: glory. The glory both Spartans lived for. They had fought this enemy – the Tegeans – before. They were fierce opponents.

With a nod to his brother, Thorakis pushed his shield high on to his shoulder, and gripped the reins tightly.

'For the Dioscuri!' he cried, calling on the twin gods most sacred to Spartans.

'For Kastor and Polydeukes!' shouted back Demokrates.

Both men kicked their heels into the stallions' sides, and galloped over the hilltop, scattering rocks and loose soil.

They plunged into the fight. The massed ranks of Spartan soldiers – the phalanx – were still in order, but reduced, and the Tegeans threatened to break through at any moment. Across the ground lay a tangle of wounded, dying and dead bodies, and the torn, muddied scarlet cloaks of fallen Spartan infantry.

The sky darkened. Thorakis heard his brother shout out – *Archers!* He raised his shield above his head. With a sound like deafening hail, arrows buried themselves in the bronze. Thorakis's elbow buckled under the deadly shafts, and he bent his knees to take the strain. Beside him, Demokrates was already bearing down on one of the enemy, a Tegean soldier from the north. With an overarm thrust of his spear, the man fell with a cry and

2

was trampled beneath the hooves of Demokrates' horse.

Then the Spartan phalanx broke. Enemy soldiers poured through the gap in the line.

'Demokrates!' yelled Thorakis. 'Fill the breach!'

If they could not drive back the enemy, the battle was lost. Instinctively, Thorakis reached inside his cloak, his fingers brushing the amulet that hung there – the Fire of Ares, God of War. It had been in his family for generations, since the age of heroes. The red stone that shone in the centre of the amulet was the only talisman he relied upon.

Thorakis picked out the largest of the enemy soldiers, a giant of a man who swung two axes above his head. Releasing the pendant, Thorakis felt adrenalin flood his veins. He lowered his short sword and pointed it towards the Tegean. Their eyes met, and Thorakis prepared to charge.

But suddenly a curious sensation, cool at first, then molten, spread through his belly. His strength leaked away. Looking down, his vision blurred through a veil of pain. Thorakis saw that the tip of a sword had pushed through his tunic at his stomach. 'Stabbed from behind,' he muttered, his voice cracking. He had seen enough of death to know that the wound was mortal – he would not make it from the battle plain alive. Never again would he see his homeland or his love, nor would he see his unborn son. But worse, he might be thought a coward.

3

Thorakis slipped from the saddle like a loose sack of grain, and hit the ground with a heavy thud. Waves of pain coursed along the length of the blade in his belly.

Helpless, he watched as the hulking enemy soldier approached and knelt down, pulling a dagger from his belt. *Let this be quick*, prayed Thorakis. The cold blade rested against his neck. But the killing thrust never came. With a twist of his wrist, the Tegean jerked Thorakis's leather thong away from his neck. He climbed to his feet, clutching the Fire of Ares in a dirty, bloodstained fist. It must have become visible in the fall! As he watched the soldier lift the amulet to his face, Thorakis's vision faded even more. Colour drained away. All colour but the one red stone.

Over the din of the raging battle, he heard a new sound. His ancestors, brave warriors before him, were calling him towards the Underworld. He felt one foot in this life, and one in the next. *Not yet*, he thought, *I must rescue the Fire of Ares!* But he could not pull himself up.

A sudden flash of scarlet.

Demokrates appeared and lunged forward, plunging his eight-foot spear into the Tegean's neck. The warrior's face registered shock, before his eyes rolled white and he collapsed to the floor. He was dead before his face hit the dusty plain.

Demokrates pulled the Fire of Ares from the corpse's fingers, and fell to his knees at Thorakis's side. Tears welled in Demokrates' eyes as he carefully eased off his brother's helmet.

'Do not weep for me,' croaked Thorakis. 'Tell others that I died facing the enemy. I will enter Sparta with honour, on my shield. When my soul embraces my father's over the River Styx, I will be in good company.' He coughed as the blood welled up in the back of his throat. 'Keep safe the Fire of Ares, Demokrates, and give it to my son when he is born. Do this for me.'

Through the growing shadow of unconsciousness, Thorakis felt Demokrates heave him on to his saddle and gallop from the battlefield.

His death came softly like the waves of the Aegean at sunset.

CHAPTER 1

'That's fifty. Stop now!' Lysander heard from behind. He let his sickle drop on to the sheared stalks. Stretching to his full height, the muscles of his back lengthened, and he turned to face his friend Timeon, who was tying a bundle of barley. The sun still blazed high in the sky. The day was sweltering, and the Taygetos Mountains shimmered in the distance. No breeze swept the plain and he could hear the trickle of the River Eurotas nearby.

Fifty already! A full day's toil even for a grown man. Lysander tipped back his head to swallow a mouthful of water from his flask, before offering it to his friend. His long locks, heavy with sweat, begin to cool against his neck.

'You must slow down,' urged Timeon, walking up to take a drink.

'You know I can't,' replied Lysander, 'not today.' He paused, looking across the fields all around them. They were dotted with other slaves harvesting the crops of the Spartan Prince Kiros. He made a rough calculation in his head. 'Another fifty before sunset will be enough.'

Timeon spluttered on his drink.

'Listen, Lysander, how can you help your mother if you have sunstroke?'

Lysander had known Timeon since before they could walk. After twelve years of friendship, he was the closest thing to a brother Lysander had.

'Fifty bushels will only buy us food,' said Lysander, 'and she needs more medicine if she is to recover.' He could see that his friend wanted to argue, but was holding back. Two of Timeon's cousins had already been taken by the wasting disease.

'Fifty more,' he said again to himself, tying the flask back to his side.

Fifteen bushels later and Lysander's body was begging for rest, but he resisted. *Don't stop*, he ordered himself. The handle of the heavy sickle was smeared with blood from the open blisters that stung his palms. He ignored the pain. It wasn't the Spartan way to whimper, to complain, or to give in. Spartans endured. Lysander imagined himself as a Spartan foot soldier in the heat of battle, pressing forward against the enemy, one step at a time; the sickle, his spear, cutting down his foe.

But Lysander wasn't a Spartan. He wouldn't even be allowed to speak to a Spartan without being spoken to first. He was a Helot, a native with no rights, no future, lower than a Spartan's dog. Each year the five Spartan Ephors – the Guardians – declared a ritual war on the Helots who lived in their midst, each year they pledged to prolong the slavery.

Lysander watched the tendons of his arms tighten and relax as he swung the sickle through the dry barley. Anger gathered in the well of his chest, and burned red like the stone that lay against his breastbone – the Fire of Ares. He had worn the pendant for as long as he could remember. He feared that if a Spartan ever saw the brilliant red jewel, he would be sure to lose it – by law, Helots had no property of their own. The Spartans could take anything they chose to. Lysander's mother, Athenasia, had always been secretive about the amulet: *Do not ask where it comes from. Just keep it close and keep it secret.* Not even Timeon knew it hung there.

Two black crows flapped up out of the barley ahead. Among the tall stalks something pale caught Lysander's eye. He stopped swinging the sickle.

'What is it?' panted Timeon, some distance behind him.

'I don't know,' replied Lysander, walking over to investigate.

As he drew closer, his steps slowed and his heart sped up. The pale object was a hand, and he recognised the body that went with it.

'It's Cato,' he called to Timeon. Lying on his back facing the sky, Cato might have been asleep if it weren't for the ragged red gash across his throat. The birds had obviously been at his eyes. Timeon came up alongside him and looked down. He lunged away and was violently sick. A few rows over, someone must have heard his retching. A lighthearted shout came across: 'What have you found there, friends?'

It wasn't long before a crowd of harvesters had gathered around the corpse. Nestor, an older man who lived near Lysander and his mother, was first to speak.

'It must be the Krypteia,' he said grimly. *Krypteia* – the word made Lysander's throat feel tight. The Spartan death squads were part of life as a Helot, though thank Zeus he had never met them. They roamed the territories at night, looking for easy prey and practice in killing. Although neither he nor Timeon had been close to Cato, Lysander knew that he had been lively and hard-working, even if he had one too many harsh words about their Spartan masters. He had obviously been overheard and paid the price.

'What shall we do with him?' asked Lysander.

'Nothing, until the overseer returns,' replied Nestor. 'We'll take him to the road for now.'

At Nestor's command, two young Helots picked up Cato's body by the shoulders and knees, and carried him away. One by one, the crowd returned to their work. Nestor was the last to go but, as he left, he turned back to Lysander.

'How does your mother fare?' he asked.

'She's no worse,' he replied.

Nestor gave a small, slow nod.

'Well, thanks to the Gods for that,' he muttered, before walking away.

Lysander focused on the harvesting, though he could not shake off the image of the dead man, with the awful second smile under his chin.

He barely noticed the rest of the afternoon pass. He swung the sickle back and forth, fuelled by his frustration and rage, until a voice interrupted his thoughts. It was Timeon.

'Lysander, slow down. You already have one hundred bushels.'

Lysander breathed out heavily, put his hands on his hips and looked up at the sun. It was a rich orange smudge a few finger widths above the mountains to the west. Hundreds of years ago, before Prince Kiros was even born, all the land between those hills and the western sea had belonged to Lysander's people. They had reaped the crops they sowed and lived in peace. Back then they were free.

Lysander heaved the last of his bushels on to the overseer's cart, then watched in silence as Nestor and another man, with their jaws set hard, lifted Cato's lifeless body carefully on to the back. They straightened out his crooked legs, and tucked in an arm that swung loosely over the side. A solitary fly buzzed over one of the dried red eye sockets, and Nestor waved it away. With a smack of the overseer's whip, the two oxen pressed into their halters and the cart jolted forward. Lysander walked behind with the other Helots, trying not to look at the grim cargo. He was glad that no one was talking.

At the barn they joined the queue of Helots waiting for their wages – a tenth of what they had harvested that day. The rest went straight to the Spartans. *But I'm one of the luckier ones*, thought Lysander, surveying the other workers. Some of the men and women were old and bent, and still expected to labour in the fields. Their sagging faces wore a look of defeat.

Lysander's stomach was growling with hunger by the time he reached the front of the line and faced the overseer, Agestes. He was a brute of a man, with coarse dark hairs matting his chest and arms, and an untidy black beard covering most of his jaw and cheeks. His small, squinting eyes glinted black, and under his thick moustache Lysander saw rotting gums and barely a tooth left in his head. He had only recently taken on the job of overseer, but already had a reputation for cruelty. On his first day he'd made an example of one of Nestor's sons, breaking his left wrist with a thresher after he asked for more water. Lysander held out his hand to receive his wages, but only one small sack of grain was thrown on to the table in front of him.

'Next!' shouted the overseer. Lysander stood for a moment. *There must be a mistake*, he thought.

'That is not enough,' he protested. 'I am owed at least twice as much.'

Agestes narrowed his eyes and leant forward, so close that Lysander could smell his sour breath. 'Move along,' ordered the overseer, the aggression etched in his face.

'But we cut one hundred today,' Lysander explained. 'I worked through the midday sun to bring in my mother's share as well.'

The overseer smiled insincerely.

'I need the extra grain to trade for her medicine – she is very ill.'

The overseer made a show of looking at the empty space on Lysander's right and left.

'I can't see your mother here, boy,' he said, folding his arms.

I'm being made a fool of! thought Lysander.

'I told you,' said Lysander, trying to control the anger in his voice. 'She is too ill to work – she's coughing blood – that is why I laboured like an ox in the fields today.'

Lysander heard gasps come from the Helots stood behind him. Agestes's smile clouded over.

'Well, Helot worm, tell your mother that she can have her grain when she comes here and gets it herself.'

A hand at his side caught Lysander's attention. It was Timeon. His eyes were full of fear. 'Come on, Lysander. We ought to go.'

The overseer was a free-dweller; still not a Spartan citizen, but one rung above a Helot. He could do as he pleased with slaves.

Behind Lysander, the other field workers were becoming impatient. He could hear grumbles of 'Move along!' and 'We want to get home'. But he did not budge.

'I am feeling generous today, young one,' the overseer said. He seemed to be thinking. 'You can take the full quota of grain, but on one condition. You take six lashes. My arm is in need of some practice.'

Lysander was no stranger to the harsh bite of a whip.

He didn't hesitate.

'I'll take the lashing.'

Lysander was led by the overseer over to the wall of the barn, where a huge cartwheel stood upright, awaiting repair.

'Strip, Helot!' barked Agestes, uncoiling the whip from his side and flexing his arm. Lysander slowly pulled his tunic down over his shoulders, slipping the Fire of Ares safely out of sight in the folds. The overseer bound his wrists to two of the wheel's spokes, wide apart. Lysander told himself that Spartan boys went through this many times as part of their brutal training. The crowd from the queue gathered to watch. Even though Lysander was one of their own, he could feel the other Helots' eyes drilling into his back.

Lysander bowed his head. He could hear the overseer shift his feet in the dirt, establishing his position.

Anything a Spartan can take, so can I, thought Lysander, gritting his teeth.

'I am ready. Do what you –' His words were interrupted by the crack of the whip across his shoulder blades. At first, all Lysander sensed was the sudden cold of the leather across his back. But then came the pain, as the burning spread out in prickles like a thousand pins simultaneously driven into his flesh. His vision went white, and he tasted the iron tang of blood where he was biting down into his lip. He managed not to cry out. The crowd roared, 'One!'

As each blow fell, Lysander shrank deeper into himself, becoming more mind than body. His heartbeat slowed and the noises of the jeering mob grew distant. He concentrated on the pendant that blazed under his clothes. Its red glow seemed to give him strength and hope. One day he would escape slavery. He would take himself and his mother away from this place, where his once-proud people were made to toil by Spartans too proud to work the land themselves. He would taste freedom.

By the time the last stroke fell, the crowd's bloodlust had subsided. Only a few of them murmured, 'Six.' His hands were untied, but still gripped the wheel rim like stiff claws. Lysander's legs threatened to give way beneath him. The evening breeze that gusted through the yard made the broken skin of his back throb, and the blood pooled in the folds of fabric around his waist. He pulled his tunic back up without a grimace, walked over to the overseer's table and seized two bags of grain — his by right all along.

'Taken like a true Spartan,' scoffed Agestes, but the overseer could not meet Lysander's eye.

CHAPTER 2

The horizon burned red with the setting sun. The strength returned to his legs, Lysander lengthened his stride and marched towards the outskirts of Limnae, one of the five villages that made up the central district of Sparta. Timeon, whose head came only a little above Lysander's shoulder, struggled to keep pace alongside. They passed the street vendors who lined the roads, trying to sell the last of the day's wares. *Ripe watermelons – perfect after a day in the fields! Roasted hazelnuts – only three bags left!* Normally, Lysander would have stopped and shared a joke or two, but not today.

'You should let my mother look at those wounds,' Timeon said nervously. 'They might become infected.'

'I'm fine,' replied Lysander, pressing on. His back stung like it was being held too close to a fire, hot and itchy. Every now and then, his tunic pulled away from where it was caked to the drying wounds. Each time, Lysander had to dig his nails into his palms and try not to whimper. There was not much time to get to the physician's store before it closed, and he needed his mother's medicines.

'Agestes won't forget this day,' said Timeon. 'I wish you had seen his face when you didn't cry out – like the blacksmith God Hephaistos hammering at a stubborn piece of iron.'

Lysander was pleased that Timeon could not see his face in the failing light. He knew his cheeks were flushed with shame. *Where is the honour in courage*, he thought, *if it comes with humiliation?* He did not want to talk about it.

The medicine store was attached to the front of the physician's house, some distance from the centre of the village. As they neared the door, Timeon tried a final time to break the silence.

'And the other men, they respected you. Not many of them would have stood up to the overseer like that.'

Lysander rounded on his friend.

'Don't be so foolish, Timeon. The other men don't respect me. They laughed and jeered through it all. Because I don't deserve respect. I . . . and you . . . we are slaves, Timeon. We own nothing. Not even our own bodies. We are worthless. Don't you understand?'

Timeon looked up at him, but then let his eyes drop. Lysander's blood quickly cooled. They were outside the medicine shop.

'I'm tired of being called a Helot, a slave. I'm a Messenian, Timeon. So are you. The land over the mountains once belonged to us, and our people lived

17

in peace. They were brave when they had to be, but otherwise they grew their crops and reared their live-stock, and they were happy. Now we're forced to work the land of a Spartan prince. Do you never wonder what it would be like to be free, as our ancestors were, before the Spartans invaded our land?'

Timeon met his gaze once again, and gave a brief smile, before speaking slowly and deliberately.

'Of course I do, but I don't dwell on it. I was born a Helot, Lysander, just like you. Hope is a dangerous thing.'

Lysander leant forward and put his hand on Timeon's shoulder. He spoke his next words more quietly.

'I'm not the only one who dares to hope, my friend. You know of the Resistance as well as I. All the men are talking about it. They meet at night. I have heard them near our house. It's said they are waiting for the perfect opportunity to strike. We don't have to accept this fate, Timeon. Every year the Ephors declare their war on us. But one day we will throw off our chains. I only hope I can play my part.'

'Just don't end up like Cato,' Timeon said. Then he seemed to think for a moment, before continuing. 'And what makes you think the Spartan lot is any better? Spartan boys are beaten often. And even if some die in this *training*, they think it makes the rest stronger by example. It's madness to want to be like that!' As usual, Timeon knew how to reason with him. Lysander brought his hand up to Timeon's shoulder and gave a friendly squeeze.

'I'm sorry, my friend, today has tested me more than usual. Come, let's go in.'

The interior of the physician's shop was gloomy, lit only by the fire that blazed at the far side of the room. Several cooking pots hung at different heights over the bank of flames, and the air was filled with woody smells. Sacks of powders and dried plants sat along the back wall, and the shopkeeper stood over the counter, pounding a concoction with a pestle and mortar. He eyed the two boys over his hooked nose.

'And what can I do for two Helots?' he asked, showing the sparkle of silver in his two top teeth. The owner was another free-dweller. Spartans were forbidden to take on any trades. Their lives were dedicated to war, and war alone. It was the free-dwellers and Helots who ran the markets and kept society functioning.

'I need some more medicine for my mother,' replied Lysander. 'The last batch doesn't seem to have helped – she's still sick.'

'She still lives, though,' smirked the shopkeeper. 'I would say the medicine has worked well indeed.' He chuckled at his own joke, and Lysander clenched his jaw. The physician noticed the look on his face.

'We'll try something else, then.' Reaching into an earthenware jug, he measured out a small pile of dark leaves. 'This is black hellebore. You'll need to crush a small handful of these with sap from poppy seeds, then bring the mixture to boil in some water. The hellebore should help her chest, and the poppy will ease her pain and help her sleep. It will not taste nice, but then what do the Spartans say? *Do not trust a doctor who prescribes honey.*'

'I wouldn't trust a free-dweller at all,' whispered Timeon, under his breath. Lysander suppressed a smile.

When the owner had wrapped the precious leaves in a small cloth bag, he placed it on his side of the counter.

'And now, for payment?' he enquired.

'I have grain,' offered Lysander, holding up one of his sacks.

The owner reached over and took it from Lysander's hand, peering inside.

'Very good,' he said, pausing to look into Lysander's other hand, 'and that one as well.'

Lysander was not sure if he had heard correctly.

'But . . . but last time it was only one, and that was expensive! The price can't have doubled in a week.'

The physician slammed his fist down on to the counter, upsetting the pestle and mortar and sending seeds scattering across the floor. Timeon let out a gasp.

'Listen, boy, these ingredients are more expensive and I've got grain enough to fill Mount Olympus,' he spat. 'When you start paying in proper currency – iron – like everyone else, then *you* can dictate prices to *me*. Now pay what you owe or take your filthy Helot grain out of my shop and watch your mother die!'

20

For a moment, Lysander thought of grabbing the medicine and running, but the look on Timeon's face convinced him otherwise. Whereas Spartan children were encouraged to steal as part of their survival training, life as a Helot was very different. If Lysander was caught, death was almost certain. Lysander placed his other sack of grain on the table and took hold of the wrapped medicine.

'Let's go home,' he said to Timeon.

It was dark as the two friends parted company outside a baker's. The smell of fresh bread made Lysander's mouth water. He knew that there were only stale crusts waiting for him at home, probably spotted with blue and green mould. He said farewell to Timeon, gripping his forearm, as was the Helot custom. His friend leant forward and spoke in his ear.

'Remember what I said, Lysander. We have to do the best with what we've got — each other and our families.' As he drew away, he pressed a small bag of his own grain into Lysander's hand. Timeon started to walk away, but called back over his shoulder, 'Don't worry, my family are all working. You need it more than us.'

Tears of gratitude gathered in the corners of Lysander's eyes. But there was also sadness: Timeon's close family were all alive and in good health. Lysander and his mother had only each other. His father was dead even before he was born. He shook himself and set off to buy provisions.

Most of the stalls in the centre of Limnae had closed up for the night, so all Lysander managed to get was some bread, hard green olives and dried fish. Still, it was enough. Lysander made for home in the dark. The sky was cloudless and the stars twinkled in clusters. As he scanned the sky, Lysander picked out the brightest constellation: Kastor and Polydeukes. The Spartans called them the *Dioscuri*, the Twins. *If all Greece worshipped the same gods, why aren't all Greeks equal?* wondered Lysander. He uttered a prayer under his breath, the same one as always: 'Warrior sons of Zeus, let me be free.'

With a last glance at the night sky, Lysander set off towards a short cut he knew beside the slaughterhouse. He could not remember the last time he and his mother had been able to afford fresh meat. But maybe Timeon was right. Perhaps life was not as bad as he thought. With the medicine, his mother would get better and be able to work again; they would bring in more money . . .

Suddenly, a voice came out of the shadows.

CHAPTER 3

'Surround him,' said the voice, laughing. 'This one is dangerous, boys!'

Lysander poked his head around the corner of the slaughterhouse and peered into the gloomy alley. He saw a group of three young men gathered around a smaller boy, who held out a piece of wood with his shaking hand.

'Stay back,' he said, thrusting the stick through the air.

Draped in their distinctive red cloaks, it was clear the gang was made up of Spartans. One was bigger than the others. He seemed to be giving the orders:

'We'll have to take his legs. A soldier can't fight when he is on the ground.' He gestured to a stocky friend. 'Ariston, you're next.'

A Spartan stepped forward. The small boy was probably a free-dweller caught in the wrong place at the wrong time. He shifted his feet to meet his new attacker. He clearly lacked any training. His arms and legs were thin, and he swung the stick wildly, but all the time the Spartan called Ariston easily managed to keep out of range.

'I haven't done anything to —' said the small free-dweller.

Without warning, Ariston dived at the boy's legs and sent him flying on to the ground. Dust flew up as the rest of the pack waded in.

Lysander could not stand and watch any more. He stepped into the alley.

'Stop that!' he called out.

The Spartans paused in their attack. Lysander watched the young men turn in his direction.

The world seemed to shrink, and Lysander felt very alone.

The large Spartan, the leader, stared at Lysander as though he was something he'd scraped off his shoe.

'A Helot pig out after dark! That could be dangerous.'

All attention was on Lysander now, and the younger boy took advantage of the distraction to scuttle down the far end of the alley. One of the Spartan gang gave chase, but their leader shouted to let him go.

'We have another hare to hunt now,' snarled the Spartan with a flash of white teeth.

Lysander turned to go back the way he had come, but saw to his dismay that two more Spartans, both lean and wiry, blocked that end of the alley.

'Have I missed any sport, Demaratos?' one of them asked.

'Not at all, Prokles,' said the leader. 'You've missed the first course. Now we have this Helot pig as the main dish.'

Ariston spoke next.

'Yes, and we all know what happens to pigs out after dark.'

Panic rose in Lysander's chest as the alleyway filled with young men, three at one end, two at the other. As the two groups closed in on him, one word pounded inside Lysander's head: *Krypteia*. Was he going to die here, in this dingy alley? *You fool*, he cursed himself, *you should have kept out of this.*

But as the five approached, the silver glance of the moonlight revealed that they could not be an experienced murder squad. They were Spartan boys of about his own age. Lysander was relieved, but knew he was still far from safe. As a Helot, his life was worth nothing to them. The leader, Demaratos, was tall and broad, with fierce eyes and a mouth that naturally curled to a sneer. His black hair was cut short and neat, and his cloak hung off muscular shoulders.

'You have to pay the tax to walk our streets, Helot,' he demanded. His eyes travelled up and down Lysander, measuring him up. 'What do the bags hold?'

Lysander knew his only option was to try and talk his way out of trouble; anything else would be suicide. He wished Timeon were here. People joked that he could talk his way out of the Underworld given half a chance.

'Look,' he said, trying to calm the tremor in his voice, 'I've got nothing, just some food, some scraps of food and medicine for my mother. She's very ill, and I need to give it to her as soon as possible.'

'Show me,' ordered the boy, motioning towards the bag of medicine that he had tucked in his belt. Lysander had no choice. He untied the small sack and held it out. The Spartan boy snatched the precious bag of leaves. He tore the twine off and glanced inside. He was clearly disappointed with his plunder, and the other boys were looking bored now, too. Lysander began to feel the tide turn in his favour.

'OK, comrades, leave him be,' said the leader, handing back the medicine. But just as Lysander reached out to take the sack, the Spartan youth let go of it. The contents fell to the ground, mingling with the dust.

The gang broke out into raucous laughter, slapping each other's backs. Lysander could have walked away then if he had wanted. But something made him stay where he was. He felt lightheaded, but strong and reckless.

'You shouldn't have done that,' he said quietly.

The group stopped laughing, one by one. The leader looked straight at Lysander. He took a step closer and bowed his head a little, cupping his ear with a hand.

'What did you say, Helot pig?'

The hairs prickled along the back of his neck.

'I said, you shouldn't have done that,' he repeated,

louder this time.

All the good humour had disappeared from the Spartan's eyes. They became as cold and dark as the night air.

'This Helot pig must think himself as mighty as Herakles. I think it is time we spiked him, don't you, comrades? After all, we are beside the slaughterhouse.'

No one laughed at the coincidence; the mood was deadly serious. Lysander caught a movement to his right as a blade flashed in the hand of the short boy. He had to think quickly. These were Spartan apprentices, trained in killing. If he hung back they would make short work of him; he had to attack first.

He feinted towards the leader on his left, before launching himself the other way, straight at the Spartan wielding the knife. His fist connected against the boy's slack, open jaw, sending him reeling to the ground. The knife flew from the Spartan's hand and landed out of sight. The second of the pair barely had time to react, before he too was doubled over by a kick from Lysander. He fell to the floor with an 'Umph!', the wind knocked out of him. Lysander was taking no chances with the other three. He saw the gap he had created and set off towards the end of the alleyway, fast.

But then his good fortune ran out. He felt a tightening around his neck – the Fire of Ares! Someone must have grabbed the leather strap. Before he could do anything to prevent it, the tension gave way. Lysander skidded to a halt and twisted around.

'Looking for this?' teased the Spartan leader, swinging the amulet back and forth on the frayed leather thong. The two others picked themselves up, the shorter boy wiping blood from his mouth.

He heard his mother's voice in his head: *Never take off the amulet – keep it safe. Always.* He had no choice. He couldn't lose the Fire of Ares.

He threw himself headlong at the leader, bowling him to the floor and trapping him between his knees. He lashed out with his fists and elbows, not caring if he missed a few times. He felt one of the others slip an arm around his neck, and while he tried to free himself, the leader drove a punch into one of his kidneys. Lysander crumpled and was thrown off. Blows soon came from every angle, as the other gang members punched and kicked his stomach, face, sides and back. Soon there was no pain, and no noise, just calm acceptance.

He was finished.

'Stop at once!' came a voice. It had such authority that Lysander wondered if a god had spoken. 'I said – *Stop!*'

The hammer of blows slowed and then ceased altogether. Lysander stayed curled in a defensive ball as the pain returned, flowing through every limb.

'What in the names of Kastor and Polydeukes is going on here?'

Lysander opened his eyes slowly – at least one of the lids was already swelling up. He made out a shape approaching. As he let his body relax, the shape became a man, standing over him and holding a flaming torch. Nearby, in the dust, Lysander spotted the Fire of Ares, and scrambled over to grab it. Once it was back in his hand, he felt safe. *Did the older man see the pendant?* He didn't know. His attention was focused on the gang of youths, who all looked terrified.

'Is this what your training has taught you?' the man demanded, his voice full of disgust. 'To take on one defenceless boy in the dead of night when no one can hear him cry out?'

The boys looked at Demaratos for an answer. After considering for a moment, he took a step forward.

'But he's just a –' he began.

'Just a what?' cut in the stranger. 'Just a Helot?' He waited a moment for his words to sink in. 'He hasn't wronged you. He poses you no threat. Yet you set on him like a pack of jackals. Your mothers should have left you on the slopes of Mount Taygetos. What are you doing out of the barracks?'

The boys looked at each other. They clearly didn't have an answer.

'Get back there immediately, unless you want this incident to reach your trainer's ears?'

Respect for one's elders was a cornerstone of Spartan society, and Lysander knew enough of Spartan discipline to know that misbehaviour was severely punished.

'Get out of my sight!' roared the man. The boys

turned and fled out of the alleyway. Their leader followed last of all, walking backwards and staring at Lysander.

'This is not over,' he whispered.

A voice came from one of his comrades at the end of the alley: 'Come on, Demaratos! He's nothing.'

A few seconds later, Lysander was alone with the Spartan warrior.

'Are you badly hurt?' he asked, leaning down to offer his hand. Lysander was too afraid to take it. Crouching on the floor, he scrambled about, picking up the leaves for his mother's medicine. The food lay trampled into the ground, so he salvaged what he could. He glanced up at the man in the light of the torch. The man was tall, and despite being at least sixty, his back was unbent and his legs looked solid with muscle. A dark cloak draped from his shoulders and almost brushed the ground. He had long greying curls, hanging loose, and a great black beard, also flecked with white. A deep pale scar extended by the side of his left eye and many other smaller ones were scattered across his face.

'I am Sarpedon,' continued the Spartan. He spoke as though the name should mean something. Lysander climbed gingerly to his feet. None of his bones seemed to have been broken in the beating.

'You are not so talkative, I see,' grunted the old man. 'A Spartan trait.' He paused, looking up the alley to where the gang had fled. 'The Spartan upbringing is hard on children, and it takes them time to learn when they should fight, and when they should be peaceful. Be assured, their lessons will be painful.'

Lysander smiled.

'Tell me, Helot, what do you know of a Spartan soldier called Thorakis?'

'Nothing,' said Lysander, 'nothing, at all. I am a Helot, a field worker . . .' But the name did mean something to him – it sent a shiver through him that he did not understand. *What does that name mean?* he thought.

'Well, then,' Sarpedon continued, gesturing with a hand. Lysander noticed that two fingers were missing beyond the second knuckle – no doubt a memento of battle. 'Tell me instead about that jewel I saw on the ground.' Lysander fought to keep the fear out of his face. 'Come now, don't be difficult. I despise thieves as much as bullies.'

Lysander gripped the amulet even tighter. His mother's words echoed in his head: *Keep it close. Keep it secret.* Could he escape one old man if he had to?

'I'm not a thief,' he heard himself shout out. 'The amulet was a gift from my mother.' He cursed himself. *I've already given too much away.*

'And nor am I,' Sarpedon assured him. 'I wish only to see it a little closer. I give you my word as a Spartan.'

There was something in the old man's voice that reassured Lysander. The weight of the day's ordeals fell upon him. Weariness hung on his limbs, and he knew he could not face any more struggles. He dropped the pendant into the warrior's scarred hand.

Sarpedon lifted the amulet to his face, and gazed at it for a long while with his head bowed. Would he take it, after all? thought Lysander. Lysander's breath caught in his chest. What would his mother say? Would she believe him, or think he had lost it carelessly in the fields?

With deliberate care, Sarpedon handed the jewel back. Lysander breathed again.

'And where did a Helot find an object of such beauty?' he asked. There was no threat in his tone, but it was not a question Lysander could answer. He had already said too much. He started to edge along the wall in small shuffles, away from the Spartan warrior.

'I . . . I have to go now,' said Lysander.

'Do not flee. I mean you no harm.' Sarpedon took a step towards him, but that was enough. Lysander turned and ran.

CHAPTER 4

Lysander tripped on the path, sprawling in the dirt. He picked himself up, ignoring the stinging pain, and plunged on through the darkness. Only when he reached the edge of the Helot settlement did he stop. His legs couldn't carry him any further. Fear had kept him going, but as the knocking in his chest softened, the agony returned, and cramp seized his legs. Until it passed there was nothing he could do but bite his lip and massage the knotted muscles.

Eventually, he threaded his way among the maze of low dwellings that his people called home. The settlement had hardly changed as he grew up; it was little more than a collection of low mud huts near the river. The air was heavy with the smell of animals and unwashed people. All was silent after the hard day in the fields.

Now his panic had settled, Lysander was left with shifting clouds of worry: *Was I followed? Could that scarred old Spartan find out where I live?* Lysander remembered the jewel gripped firmly in his fist – the Fire of Ares. He uncurled his stiff fingers, gazing at the amulet in his palm. *I very nearly lost it*, he thought. The red stone looked almost black now, flecked white in the moon's glare. He pushed it deep into the fold of his tunic. Placing his palm on the rough wood of the door, he gathered himself, and stepped inside.

It was warm in the single room of the shack, and his skin tingled. The embers of a weak fire smouldered in the grate.

'Mother?' he whispered, trying to control his heavy breathing. There was no answer. Lysander crept towards the fire, to where his mother's bed nestled against the wall. He had built the frame himself from scraps of stolen wood. The doctor had said that such a sick woman should not be sleeping on the packed earth of the floor. The bed had been moved as near as possible to the fire in recent months, in the hope that the flames might purge the illness in her chest. As he stepped closer, Lysander's pulse quickened – the bed did not look right. He patted the blankets, but the bed was empty. His eyes flashed around the room, straining against the gloom, but she was nowhere to be seen.

Lysander ran outside. The night was like a black lake, and his thumping heartbeat was the loudest sound he could hear.

'Mother?' he hissed. His only reply was the chattering of the cicadas that lived in the low scrub around the encampment. Then louder, 'Mother!' There was a grumble of protest from one of the nearby huts.

His chest grew cold with panic, as he shouted as loud as he could:

'Mother, where are you?'

A weak moan came from near the hut. *Mother!* Lysander dashed to the side of the building. There, where the stars' light could not reach, he found Athenasia. She half sat, half slumped against the mud wall, and beside her was an upturned draining dish and a scattering of lentils. There was a smear of dried blood across her temple.

He knelt beside her, and supported her head against his shoulder. She had grown so thin, it was like holding a child.

'Mother, are . . . are you hurt?' he stammered. 'What happened? Who did this to you?' The urge to cry tugged at his mouth.

'No one has harmed me, Lysander,' she began. 'Your foolish old mother did this to herself.' Lysander was confused, but his mother's voice calmed him.

'I must have tripped, I think . . .' She raised her hand to her forehead and winced. 'I knocked my head. I expect the dinner is spoiled,' she said.

Relief washed over Lysander. He could live with a ruined dinner. Carefully, he lifted his mother to her feet.

Lysander finished washing the remains of the lentils outside and stepped back inside the shack. The fire was burning once again, throwing orange shadows across the hut. The low roof would need fixing before the winter came, where the mud was cracking, and parts of the thatch had come loose.

Athenasia was resting once again on her bed. Lysander had cleaned and bandaged her head. Now he knelt beside the fire, stirring the dried medicinal leaves into a saucepan of simmering water. The steam hurt his eyes, and he had to fight back tears. His mother's condition had lasted for months now. Every day he looked for signs that she was recovering, but there weren't any. He didn't mind looking after her, but sometimes he missed his younger days when he could run around with the other boys. Those days had gone for ever.

'Why didn't you wait for me to get home?' he said. 'I can cook our supper, and you need to rest.' He paused, and looked at his mother. Her blue eyes were watery, and her skin pale, but he could still see the beautiful woman she had once been. Her high cheekbones were more prominent than they used to be, the cheeks sunken. Her once-brown hair was grey and thinning. But she still wore it long.

'I'm sorry,' she said. 'I will heed your words in future.'

Lysander smiled back. He used a cup to scoop up some of the medicine, and added a little mint oil to help with her breathing, as Timeon's mother had suggested. Crouching by the side of Athenasia's bed, he supported her head in his hand, and brought the cup slowly to her lips. She sipped a small amount, and grimaced.

Athenasia was suddenly racked with deep coughing which shook her whole body and made it impossible for her to speak. Lysander waited, sitting by her until the fit had passed. She gripped him tightly. Through the material of his tunic, her nails caught on his wounds, and he could not help the gasp of pain that escaped his lips.

'What's wrong?' asked his mother.

'Nothing,' he replied. 'Nothing at all . . . a few grazes from the fields.'

'Your eyes betray you,' said his mother. 'Show me.'

Reluctantly, Lysander pulled his tunic over his head, and turned around.

'Lysander!' she gasped. 'Who did this to you?'

'It was Agestes,' he mumbled. 'We had a . . . difference of opinion.'

'Please tell me what happened, Lysander,' she said. 'I am worried about you.'

So he told her about the reduced grain ration, and the flogging that had followed.

'Agestes is an animal,' she said. With a sigh she started to climb from her bed. Lysander got up as well. 'Stay where you are,' she said. 'I might be ill, but I can still look after you. Fetch over that stool, and sit down.' Lysander did as he was told.

His mother took a cup of warm water from the

hearth, and a cloth. She dabbed the swellings with a sponge, lifting his long hair away from his shoulders. She paused and Lysander heard a small intake of breath.

'Where is the Fire of Ares?' Her voice was panicked.

'Do not worry, Mother, it is safe,' he replied, bringing it out from his pocket. Now was not the time to tell her about the second beating of the day – it would only worry her further. 'Look, the thong is broken, that's all.'

Athenasia took the pendant and strap out of Lysander's hand and quickly retied it around his neck.

'Lysander, remember what I have always said,' she said. 'Never take off the Fire of Ares. Do you understand? Never. You must always keep it safe. Promise me.'

Lysander didn't argue or try to explain.

'Mother, I swear I'll never lose it.' Athenasia's face relaxed. 'Now finish your medicine.'

Athenasia managed only a few mouthfuls of bread and lentils, but Lysander ate all of his before finishing her leftovers. With his stomach full, he lay on his patch of ground to rest, pulling the threadbare blanket over him. Even with the fire burning, the cold still seeped in through cracks around the door. The day had been long and stressful, but his mind was not ready for sleep even though his body ached for it. In the darkness, he saw Cato's limp body as the men lifted it from the field, the brute Agestes and the greedy physician, the sneers of Demaratos and his gang of Spartan bullies. And last of all, Sarpedon. Lysander thought back to the look on the old man's face when he saw the Fire of Ares. *What did that look mean?* Was it envy? Greed? Or simply confusion that a Helot boy could possess something so beautiful?

He rolled over on to his side.

'You can't sleep?' his mother asked drowsily.

'I'll be fine,' he replied. 'Sorry to wake you.'

'What is it?'

He tried to gather his thoughts.

'Well, if there are really gods watching over us, why do they allow us to be treated this way? Why do they make the Spartans our masters? Why make us slaves?'

Athenasia was silent for a few moments, but then spoke slowly, as though she were picking her words with great care.

'Well, Lysander,' she comforted, 'just because we cannot understand the will of the Gods, that does not mean they have no plans for us.'

'And are we to simply accept what happens to us?' A dog let off a volley of barking.

'Hush, Lysander!' said his mother. 'Don't say such things.'

'Doesn't it anger you?' he whispered. 'Don't you feel there must be something more for us?'

'I know there must be, Lysander, and that is *why* I don't grow angry. Put your faith in the Gods, and they will not disappoint you. Have faith, great things await you – it is your destiny.'

'But how many Helots have placed their hope in the Fates? We Messenians have been slaves to the Spartans for nearly two hundred years. Think how many Helots have had the same thoughts as us: of freedom, of their own land! Yet the Gods have watched them live and die under the Spartan yoke. I don't believe in the Gods at all!' He turned and faced the wall.

'My poor Lysander,' said his mother. 'If you abandon the Gods, they will abandon you. The Fates have spun a bright future for you, but you must make sure you follow it. For now, try to sleep.'

Lysander woke in the middle of the night, disturbed by a noise. It sounded like something scuffing the hard earth floor. *Filthy mice*, he thought.

The fire had died to almost nothing; only a kernel of orange remained among the grey ashes. He thought about putting more logs on, but their wood was strictly rationed. Looking over to where Athenasia lay, Lysander saw that her blanket had slipped loose off her shoulder. He rose to tuck her in properly. His mother's body shivered under her coverings and a few strands of her fine hair lay plastered to her head with sweat.

Lysander gently pushed the lock of hair back from his mother's face, being careful not to wake her. Then he took his own thin blanket from around his shoulders and placed it over her.

A noise made him freeze. It sounded as though it came from in front of the hut. A scuffle of feet – probably a scavenging animal. He lay down, and brought his arms up to his chest for warmth. There was another noise, perhaps a whisper. Lysander stood and pressed his ear to the door. Beyond snatches of voices it was hard to make out. Spartan laws forbade Helots to be out of their dwellings at this hour. There could be only one explanation – another gathering. He had heard rumours. Men met in the caves by the river. The Resistance. Were they planning something soon?

Lysander longed to go out and join them. But could he? Surely they would laugh him back to bed. A thirteen-year-old boy wanting to fight the Spartans!

He listened until the sounds softened and died. It was enough to know that others longed for change as well. Thoughts of revolution and freedom flashed across Lysander's brain. He tried to imagine his own part in such a battle. As sleep drew its black cloak over his eyes, Lysander saw himself at the head of the charge against a line of Spartan soldiers, his Messenian brothers at his side.

CHAPTER 5

'Get off . . . Get away!' Lysander shouted, lashing out with his hands.

He woke with a start, panting for breath, his arms raised to protect his throat. His eyes flicked across the hut. It was empty but for the few pieces of furniture, the ashes of the fire, and his mother sleeping beneath her blankets. He sucked air into his lungs and lay back for a second. *Just a dream*, he thought, as his fingers closed around the pendant at his neck. The Fire of Ares was safe.

Lysander got up, his muscles stiff and hurting from the previous day's struggles. But he could not let that stop him. Since his mother had fallen ill, this was the only time he had to do his own, secret training. A soft light nudged under the door of their hut, and told Lysander that the sun would soon appear over the mountains to the east. He remembered the stories his mother used to tell him about the sunrise: that the great God Helios carried the sun in his horse-drawn chariot, climbing

42

each morning into the sky, then quenching his horses' thirst each evening in the western sea. But Lysander was too old for those stories now.

He was hungry, but seeing the sorry remains of their food, he decided to leave it for his mother. For a moment the anger flared again in his chest. *Is it so much to ask, enough food to feed two people who toil their guts out all day?* Kissing his mother softly on the forehead, he slipped out of the door.

The morning was still, and not a sound disturbed the cool air. Lysander looked about at the settlement. The flies were awake already, attracted by the filth of animal bones and other refuse that filled the dump nearby. The ramshackle buildings squatted in this Helot district at the edge of Prince Kiros's estate, clinging to the shallow hillside as though they had grown there. This was where his community of Messenian Helots had lived for the last fifteen years, close to the fields where they worked, but far enough from the town of the Spartans that the free-born people didn't have to smell the sewage that dried in their narrow streets.

There was a scuffle to his right, and from between two huts Timeon peered out. His straw-coloured hair was messy from sleep. His friend tiptoed over, and winced as his eyes fell on Lysander's face.

'What happened?' he whispered.

'I met some Spartans on my way home.'

'Are you sure you are well enough to train?' asked Timeon.

'Herakles did not cease after eleven labours,' answered Lysander. 'Come on.'

Even though his muscles ached for more time to recover, Lysander jogged away from the settlement with Timeon. His legs were warmed up by the time the millhouse came into view.

'Race you the rest of the way?' said Timeon.

'If you're ready to lose,' replied Lysander. 'Ready . . . go!'

Lysander sprinted off. He imagined he was in the foot race at the great Games at Olympia, held every four years for competitors from all over Greece. Every time he thought about slowing down, a make-believe crowd of spectators would spur him on. The other Helots often spoke of a famous Messenian athlete in the age of freedom, a man called Polykares. He was the quickest the Olympic stadium had ever seen, they said, quicker than any Spartan. Lysander reached the millhouse half a stride ahead of Timeon, who gave him a clap on the back.

'One day I'll beat you.' He grinned.

They let themselves into the deserted millhouse. The rest of the Helots wouldn't be up until the dawn spread its rosy fingers over the mountains. Lysander came to this place three times a week to harden and strengthen his body. One day the Resistance would need him. He might even be the leader. *I may be a Helot*, he repeated to himself, *but I will be as tough as any Spartan.*

With Timeon's help, he cleared a space from the millhouse floor. First he took one of the used granite millstones. It was bigger than his head, but he could just lift it. Lying on his back, Lysander held the rough stone in both hands and pushed it up from his chest, as Timeon counted for him. *One!* He lowered and lifted again: *Two!* He soon got into his rhythm: *Three . . . Four . . . Five . . .* After three sets of ten, the muscles in his arms were shaking badly and Lysander struggled to hold the weight even a small distance off his chest.

Though his body was unwilling, Lysander knew how to keep going. He thought of his mother lying ill in her bed in a draughty hut, he thought of Cato, killed by the Krypteia for fun, as easily as they'd slaughter a chicken for the pot. As long as his rage burned, he would be able to keep pushing himself.

Lysander detached the leather pulley from the crank axle that drove the millstones up and down. He wrapped the strap around his hand and pulled, taking the weight of the stone. *One . . . Two . . . Three . . .*

'Come on, Lysander!' shouted Timeon.

Agestes' face rose in his mind, spittle at the edges of his lips, as Timeon counted: *Four . . . Five . . .* He thought of the stocky Spartan he had punched to the floor, and imagined hitting him again and again: *Six . . . Seven . . . Eight . . . Nine . . . Ten!* Lysander reattached the pulley and sat back, the sweat dripping from his forehead on to the wooden floor and mingling with the fine film of grain dust. His mother's words came to his mind: 'Have faith, great things await you – it is your destiny.'

After saying goodbye, Timeon dashed off home for his breakfast. Gazing down into the surface of the millpond where he came to wash, Lysander saw his face for the first time since his beatings the previous day. One of his eyes was a nasty shade of green, and a red and black scab crusted his cheekbone on the opposite side. Beneath that, his top lip was split, though any swelling seemed to have disappeared. *Not pretty, but still more handsome than Agestes!* The grin that accompanied this thought hurt his mouth. Lysander plunged his hands into the cool water, shattering the reflection. He tossed the water on to his sore face and neck, cleaning off the grime of the fields and the millhouse. A sharp snap made him look up. The treetops swayed gently in the breeze.

'Hello?' he called out. 'Is anyone there?' There was no answer, just the ripple of the river as it entered the pond, and the odd patter of a cricket. He tied back his long hair, stood up and hurried back up the hill towards the field for another day of harvesting.

Timeon was waiting for him, holding the sickle, and chatting to another boy of their age. Lysander waved and started to make his way over. His training had lifted his spirits and he was full of renewed hope.

'Hey, you!' shouted the overseer. Lysander kept walking towards his friend.

'Hey, whipping-boy, I'm talking to you!'

Lysander turned and saw Agestes's ugly face bearing down on him. His body stiffened and his fists clenched.

'Are you deaf?' yelled Agestes. 'Has yesterday's performance not taught you some manners?'

'What do you want?' asked Lysander, lifting his chin to look Agestes in the eye. The overseer squinted back, and seemed to consider his options.

'Not looking good today, Helot!' he said, eyeing Lysander's face. 'We're down to our last few grain sacks. I need someone to go to the market at Limnae and buy some new ones.' He looked Lysander up and down. 'Get moving. We need forty at least.'

Lysander immediately thought of the grain he needed to buy food for himself and his mother. Every moment away from the fields would mean less payment.

'But if I have to go to market, I won't have time to earn –' Lysander began to protest.

'Well, then, the quicker you get there and back, the better,' Agestes said, sneering. 'Unless you wish to feel some more of this?' He fingered the whip that hung at his side.

Lysander turned towards the village.

Limnae had grown up around the businesses and markets run by the free-dwellers. As Lysander made his way through the district where the free-dwellers lived, he saw a few men and women going about their business – hanging washing, airing their bedclothes. They watched him with mild curiosity, inspecting the bruises and cuts. A slave boy jogged past, no doubt sent to fetch something, or deliver a message. The houses here were larger and sturdier than the tiny shack he occupied with his mother, and the gardens contained vegetables and the occasional fruit tree. In the small fields that surrounded the houses, goats and hens nosed and pecked for scraps of food. It was not the same lifestyle the Spartans enjoyed – Lysander could see their homes in the distance, nestled in the mountain foothills – but it was certainly a step up from the breadline existence of the Helots.

Hairs pricked on the back of Lysander's neck and he spun round. Was someone watching out of more than curiosity? *I must be getting paranoid*, he thought, shaking his head. But he knew now that those Spartan boys patrolled these streets. He dreaded bumping into them again. He couldn't always rely on one charitable Spartan appearing to rescue him. He continued quickly on his way, overtaking a cattle merchant driving his herd to the market. The great beasts must have come from the river, because their coats were slicked wet and the animals steamed in the rising heat of the sun. They moved aside lazily enough as Lysander pushed past. His mind was occupied with calculations: how much quicker would he have to work to make his wages today? Working in the fields was hard enough, without being an errand boy as well.

48

Then he *did* see someone. A figure – a man perhaps – darting between the cattle, crouching low. This was not his imagination. Lysander quickly ducked into a side street, and crouched by a wall. Opposite a dog cocked its head with curiosity, and watched with its tongue lolling from the side of its mouth.

'Just you stay quiet,' said Lysander under his breath. *Was it Demaratos and his thugs?*

He watched as the slow procession of bulls disappeared over the brow of the street, and all the street was calm again. Lysander strained his ears. There was definitely something there – soft footfalls. Then they stopped. Was that breathing? If it was one against one, he still had a chance. But what if the attacker was armed?

Lysander bunched his fingers into fists, took a deep breath, and readied himself to fight.

He jumped out into the street.

'Get away!' he shouted, hands raised.

But no one was there; the street was empty.

The dog scratched at its neck with a foreleg and scampered off.

CHAPTER 6

Despite the early hour, the market at Limnae was already busy. Sellers shouted their business to anyone who could hear: 'Line up for your figs. Juicy figs!'; 'Sheep bones, pig bones, beef bones. Perfect for broths.' Lysander's mouth was moist at the thought of thick, flour-fattened stew. He threaded a path among the people, past a plump young man selling charms to ward off evil or coerce the Gods: 'Bless yourselves, curse your enemies!'

The market spread out from a central square, and the stalls became more closely packed the nearer Lysander got to the square. The place was overwhelming. To his left a hosier was selling materials ranging from simple white cloth to fine linens. The rich smells of dried fish filled Lysander's nostrils as he walked past a stall where fillets lay in salt and long eels dangled from a beam, dried almost black in the sun.

There were other Helots in the market, helping the free-dwellers run their stalls or carrying out duties for their Spartan masters. The crowds became denser as Lysander reached the centre of the market, and he lost his sense of direction.

'Excuse me?' he asked a young woman. 'Do you know where I can buy some hemp sacks?'

'That way,' she nodded. 'Go past the dressmaker's and you will see it.'

Lysander set off towards the opposite street. Two beggars blocked his path. One was missing his right leg, and the other was blind.

'Can you spare some food?' one pleaded, his pale sightless eyes swivelling in their sockets.

'By the Gods, by the Gods, sir, alms for the poor!' said the other.

'I'm sorry,' replied Lysander, 'I have nothing.' The men must have been soldiers in the long wars against the Arcadians. Though the Spartans prided themselves on the greatest army in all of Greece, free-dwellers like these rarely received credit for their part in the battles.

The street was so narrow that Lysander had to muscle past people. He was finding it difficult to breathe. He started to feel trapped and panicked.

'I am looking for a stall that sells sacks,' he asked a small woman wearing an apron. 'Can you help me?'

But she pushed him aside: 'Get out of my way, slave.'

It was hot in the street, and the air seemed thick. Lysander turned to make his way back to the open space of the central square, but he was being jostled towards a space between two stalls.

'I need to get that way,' he said loudly, but a deep, accented voice whispered into his ear.

'Do what I say and you may live today,' hissed the man.

Lysander tried to turn, but a hand rough with calluses gripped his neck and pushed him hard against a wall.

'No, no, slave – you weren't listening.'

Lysander saw the knife – a simple, rough blade used by the Helots. Before he could react the cool flint was pressed against his throat. It hovered over his pulse.

'Look,' he said, 'I'll do anything you want.' He thought of the iron bar Agestes had given him. 'I . . . I have money.'

'I don't want your money!' said the voice. The hand on his neck loosened and for a moment he thought he was being released. But in a flurry, Lysander felt a hard shove in his back and his head crashed into the wall. Everything went black.

Lysander took some time to get to his feet. He touched his head, and when he drew his fingers away they were smeared in sticky blood that oozed from under his hairline. He brushed himself down, feeling the pouch where Agestes's iron bar remained safely contained. *Thank Zeus for that!* His hands clutched his chest beneath his neck. The Fire of Ares was gone!

Lysander's mind filled with panic. His legs were numb as he rushed through the crowd. He ignored the shoppers who called out complaints after him. From the centre of the square, where a spice-seller sat surrounded by sacks of bright powders and chillies hanging from a frame, Lysander turned full circle, scanning the crowd, letting his eyes dart from face to face. Despite the protests of the storeholder, Lysander stood on one of the unopened sacks and looked again. How tall was the man who had stolen the pendant? What colour was his hair? Lysander realised he had no idea. Sweat poured off his face. He felt sick in the pit of his stomach as he climbed down.

The Fire of Ares – his most precious possession – was gone without a trace.

Lysander made his way back through the crowds of buyers. *What can I tell my mother?* he thought. *I have broken my oath.* He was walking, with his head lowered, when he stumbled straight into someone. He just had time to see the shocked face of a boy roughly his own age before they both fell to the ground in a tangle of limbs. A shopper shuffled out of the way, grunting displeasure. Lysander scrambled to his feet, and looked down. The boy had tight curly hair, which was almost black.

'You should watch where you are going!' he said, rubbing his elbow. Lysander registered the red cloak the boy was wearing, and his heart missed a beat: a Spartan. This could mean serious trouble. Even looking at a Spartan the wrong way could get a Helot severely punished.

'I . . . I'm sorry,' stammered Lysander. 'I didn't see you.' He offered an arm.

'I do not need a Helot's help,' said the boy, and began to climb to his feet. Only then did Lysander notice the Spartan's leg where his cloak had fallen open. The right was normal, but the left . . . it was obviously thinner and a little shorter too. A patch of wrinkled, paler skin spread along the top of his knee, and the whole leg was twisted so that the foot pointed slightly inwards. Lysander let his gaze rest a moment too long and caught a flicker of shame across the Spartan's face. He pulled back the edge of red cloak quickly.

'Keep your sympathy to yourself,' said the Spartan. Lysander caught sight of the rod in the Spartan's hand. The other boy raised his hand suddenly and Lysander flinched, putting up his arms to protect himself. No blow came.

'What are you doing?' said the boy in the cloak.

Lysander lowered his defence.

'I . . . I thought you were going to beat me,' he replied.

The Spartan laughed. 'This is my walking stick. What good would it do to break it over your head?' He paused. 'What's your name?'

Lysander was speechless. He had never been asked such a personal question by a Spartan.

'You do have a name? I am Orpheus.'

'Lysander,' he replied.

'Well, Lysander, why the hurry?'

'My apologies, I . . . I'm looking for . . .' He checked himself.

The boy in the red cloak held up his hands, to calm Lysander.

'Listen, Lysander, you look terrible.' Lysander remembered the bruises and scrapes that covered his face. 'Come, sit over here,' he said, pointing to a vacant bench. Lysander felt as though he was caught in a river current from which he did not have strength to escape. With the Spartan limping ahead, he threaded a path over to the edge of the market square. He took a seat beside Orpheus, taking care to keep a respectful distance and not look the Spartan in the eye.

'Not seen a Spartan cripple before?' said Orpheus.

Lysander didn't know how to react. Was this a trap? If this Spartan had been born with his leg like that, he shouldn't even have been allowed to live. Any Spartan baby with weakness or disease was exposed and left to die on the freezing slopes of the mountains.

'It has been like that always. But sometimes my knee aches in the morning.' He paused for a moment, then added: 'They say you can't miss what you have never had, but I don't think that is true.'

Lysander dared to raise his head. The Spartan was not looking at him, but stared into the crowd. Lysander found he felt sorry for Orpheus. It must have been hard for the boy to know that he could never be a warrior.

The owner of a nearby stall, a potter with a bald

head and great rolls of fat on his neck, leant over to see who was sitting on his bench. He scowled. Then his eyes fell on the red cloak and he turned back to his work.

'There are some benefits to being a Spartan, even a lame one!' said Orpheus, suddenly smiling. 'Now are you going to tell me what is the problem? You said you had to find something . . .'

Lysander could not help but warm to his new acquaintance. There was an honesty about him that made the red cloak seem like nothing.

'I'm looking for something that is precious to me,' he said.

'What is it?' asked the Spartan boy.

Lysander heard his mother's voice – *Keep it secret.*

'I . . . I can't tell you,' he said.

'Who took it?' the Spartan asked.

'I can't tell you that either!' said Lysander. 'Because I don't know. I was attacked from behind.' He must have sounded foolish.

'That's fine, Lysander. It is not my affair, but I may be able to help. Four eyes are better than two, surely . . .'

Orpheus was no threat, Lysander could see that. Lysander took a bold step.

'I'm looking for a pendant. It's my most treasured possession and it was stolen just before I bumped into you.'

The other boy frowned, then said, 'Well, I doubt that whoever has taken it will still be nearby, so charging around probably will not help. We need to use our brains. Bet you never thought you would hear a Spartan say that?' His openness was infectious.

'No, but I've never met a Spartan with a limp, either,' said Lysander. The words were out before he could think. He watched Orpheus for a reaction, but the smile remained.

'Our births put us both at a disadvantage,' said the Spartan, 'but to blame one's birth is an affront to the Gods. Who else knew about the pendant?'

'No one, other than my mother,' said Lysander. 'Although after yesterday . . .'

Lysander thought back to the day before – to Demaratos and his gang, to Sarpedon and his stern, scarred face. Whoever attacked him knew what they were looking for. But the knife that had been used was not iron or bronze, he was sure of that. It had been flint – a home-made, Helot knife. But why would a Helot attack him? He was one of their own. Orpheus interrupted his thoughts.

'I have to go back to my barracks. I came out only to buy a gift for my mother.' He took from a pouch a small carving of a four-legged creature, made out of green quartz. It looked like a malformed pig, with a long, drooping nose. 'It's called an elephant,' said Orpheus. 'Our barracks tutor will not be merciful if I'm late.'

Late! Lysander shot to his feet. How long had he been at the market? The overseer would be furious!

'I must go as well,' he said. Through a gap in the crowd, he spotted a stall selling hemp sacks. *How could I have missed it before?* he asked himself.

With Orpheus walking behind, Lysander approached the stall. The owner was an elderly man.

'I need forty sacks, please,' said Lysander, showing the stallholder his iron bar.

The stallholder nodded his head, and began to slowly count the hemp bags.

'Can you go any quicker?' asked Lysander. 'If I am not back soon I'll receive a flogging.'

'All in good time,' said the free-dweller, tying the sacks into two separate bundles.

'Don't worry,' said Orpheus, pointing at a cart being tied to an ass. 'You can flag a lift.'

'No free-dweller would give a ride to a Helot like me,' said Lysander.

'Perhaps not,' said Orpheus, 'but they will do it for a Spartan.' He shouted over to the driver.

'Hey, you, where are you heading?'

The cart owner glanced over in puzzlement, but when he saw Orpheus's cloak, he mended his expression.

'Down the Hyacinthine Way,' he said. He jabbed a finger at the jars that filled the bottom of his cart. 'This oil is bound for the port at Gytheio.'

'That is our way also,' said Orpheus. He didn't wait for permission. 'Come on, Lysander,' he said. 'Place your bags in the back.'

Lysander did as the Spartan told him, ignoring the look of annoyance on the owner's face. He helped Orpheus up beside him. As they settled in the back, the driver flicked his whip at the ass. The cart jolted forward, and the jars rattled against one another.

As Lysander leant against the wooden side of the cart, he gazed over at the other boy. What a strange day this was becoming. Lysander had barely spoken to a Spartan before. Now he'd made friends with one.

CHAPTER 7

As the rickety cart trundled along in the direction of Prince Kiros's estate, the thunder of hooves came from up ahead. A Spartan soldier rounded the corner ahead of them. One arm held his horse's reins, the other clutched a bundle close to his chest. The driver of the cart swerved aside just in time, and the cart juddered to a halt as one set of wheels lodged into the roadside ditch. The rider galloped past regardless, and above the sound of the horse's feet, Lysander heard the wail of a baby, and saw the wriggling of pink limbs.

He looked at Orpheus. It was obvious what was happening. The baby must be unhealthy or suffering from a disability. The Spartan was taking it to the mountains, as was the custom. Lysander remembered the look of shame on Orpheus's face when he had exposed his leg. After the horseman disappeared round a corner, the Spartan spoke.

'I know what you're thinking, Lysander. How can my people bear the sight of a boy like me?'

Lysander shook his head.

'I wasn't thinking anything –'

'As a baby, I was inspected as the custom commands,' Orpheus interrupted. 'My twisted left leg sealed my fate – death. I cannot remember, of course, but my mother told me later.'

'What happened to you?' asked Lysander.

'A soldier came to the house. My parents knew there was no sense trying to prevent the inevitable. Spartans don't know the meaning of mercy. I was taken from her arms and carried up the path into the western mountains. There the soldier left me by a rosinweed bush just as the winter snows started to fall. They reasoned that if the cold did not kill me, there were many wild animals in that region that would soon sniff me out.'

'But how could you have survived? You were just a baby!'

'Well,' continued Orpheus, 'a week later, the soldier returned the same way on a hunting trip with some men from his dining mess. They were chasing down a pack of wolves. They had already killed the lead male, and injured the female, but she had escaped into the bushes. The soldier, a man called Thyestes, dismounted from his horse and entered the thicket, his short spear ready. An injured wolf is more deadly than a healthy one.'

'What happened?' asked Lysander, leaning forward.

'Thyestes followed a trail of blood deeper into the

trees. It was one of those winter days when the sun never seems to appear. It was just a weak haze behind the white sky. The wood was dark, and up ahead he heard a low growl between the trees. It sounded as though the she-wolf was licking her wounds. He edged forward . . .'

'And?' said Lysander.

'Thyestes came to a clearing, and there he saw her. The wolf crouched in front of a small cave, her side matted with dark blood. The hairs on her neck were raised and her bared teeth were white as the snow. But Thyestes could see she was weak. One of her front legs kept buckling. Why didn't she flee, he wondered? Then he heard a sound from the cave behind, a mewling squeak. She had cubs.'

'And did he kill her, even when she had young?' asked Lysander.

'Of course he did,' said Orpheus. 'He edged as close as he dared, levelling the hunting spear. The she-wolf gave a final snarl, but it was cut short when the tip of the spear pierced between the neck and the shoulder. She died quickly.'

'But what has that to do with you?' asked Lysander.

'Thyestes drew his dagger, and crouched to go into the cave. The cubs would not be a threat. He saw there were three at the back of the cave, squirming blindly over each other. He could see their mother had brought them a recent kill. There was something pink and fleshy, perhaps a rabbit, lying right in their midst.

But as he moved closer, he could not believe his eyes. It was not food – it was a baby boy. And he was alive!'

'You?' asked Lysander, amazed.

'Indeed,' said Orpheus. 'The wolf must have suckled me like one of her own cubs. Thyestes carried me back to his hunting companions. They didn't know what to do. One said they should simply leave me there in the snow. That, after all, was what Spartan law commanded. But others said I was a miracle, and that it was the work of the Gods. In the end, they brought me back to Sparta and presented me to the council.'

'And they let you live?'

'Yes, they voted to return me to my mother. They said I must be blessed by Lykurgos, the founder of Spartan society. His name means Wolf-Worker. My mother was overjoyed and called me Orpheus, after the famous musician who visited the land of the dead in the Underworld and came back out again alive.'

Lysander was astounded. Perhaps the Gods did pay attention to mortal affairs. They had reached the turning for the barracks, and Orpheus climbed down from the back of the cart.

'Do you think you are protected by the Gods?' Lysander asked.

'Either that,' replied Orpheus, 'or I was born with the strength of a thousand Spartans! Take care, Lysander, and I wish you luck finding the pendant.'

As the cart moved off, Lysander watched Orpheus hobble away. He hoped they would meet again.

Lysander leapt off the back of the cart at the edge of Prince Kiros's estate. Shouldering the two bundles, he jogged back to the fields. There, crouching in the dirt and plucking weeds from the edges of the newly sprouted crop, was his mother. He dropped the sacks and ran to her side.

'Mother! Why aren't you resting?' He could see she was too weak to reply and tears welled in his eyes. A voice boomed from behind him:

'Because someone in your family has to earn a living!' Lysander turned to see Agestes's great bulk towering over him. He helped his mother to her feet, before rounding angrily on the overseer.

'You can see she is ill!' he shouted. 'Are you trying to kill her?'

'Do not worry about me, Lysander,' urged Athenasia.

Agestes narrowed his eyes and pulled his head back. Then he spat on the ground, close to Lysander's foot.

'I should listen to your mother, Helot,' he smirked. 'Prince Kiros needs every pair of able hands in the fields to reap the harvest. That includes lazy slaves who'd rather be tucked up in bed. Unless, of course, you want me to bring the prince himself down to the fields . . .'

Lysander was about to launch a fist straight into the overseer's sternum, but he felt his mother's hand in the middle of his back. She spoke before he could, and there was fear in her voice.

'Thank you, sir,' she said to the overseer. 'We understand perfectly. We would just like to get on with our work now.'

With a snort of disgust, Agestes turned on his heel and walked away, leaving the air behind him thick with his stench.

Lysander's face burned as he worked beside Athenasia, turning over weeds with a hoe. He could see that she was barely able to remain upright. A sickly sweat shone on her pale forehead. Shame came upon him in bursts, like arrows shot into his mind. *I can't even protect my mother! I should have killed that fat stinking hog of an overseer with my bare hands.* His mother must have seen the tortured look on his face.

'It wouldn't have helped, you know,' she began. 'Fighting only creates more fighting. The Spartans would do well to remember that.'

Letting out a weak groan, she sank to one knee. Lysander dropped the hoe and rushed to hold her shoulders as the coughing racked her body. When she stopped shaking, Lysander saw that his mother's eyes were dulled and unresponsive. He had never seen her so bad before.

'*Enough!*' said Lysander. 'I am taking you home.'

He looked round for Agestes, but he was nowhere in sight. He hoisted Athenasia's frail body into his arms. She didn't protest as he carried her out of the fields. The other Helots looked on in sympathy, but none stepped out to help. What could they do? Old Nestor, his lips pressed together, gave a small nod of the head.

On the path between the fields, Lysander saw Agestes at a distance, yelling at a group of three female Helots – Lysander recognised them as the three daughters of Hecuba, a friend of his mother's. As he watched, Agestes suddenly marched forward and swung the back of his hand across the face of the youngest, Nylix, who fell to the ground with a shriek. Her sisters cowered beside her.

There was no turning back. Lysander gritted his teeth and readied himself to face the overseer. As he drew nearer, Agestes turned and stared in disbelief. He slowly stepped into the middle of the path and folded his arms.

'You, boy, are going nowhere. And neither is your mother. Get back to work at once!'

'Not this time,' said Lysander. He lowered Athenasia, who managed to find her feet. He could feel her quaking, but instead of backing off, he took a step forward. 'I will not watch my mother die in the fields.'

Agestes raised his bear-like hand and bellowed:

'Back to work! Now!'

Lysander didn't move, and he was ready when Agestes brought down his arm. He ducked to the side but kept his foot extended. Agestes's hand hit nothing but air, and his weight carried him over Lysander's outstretched leg. He crashed to the ground. For a moment he lay fighting for breath, winded by the fall.

Picking up his mother, Lysander walked as quickly as possible in the direction of their village. Agestes didn't follow, but called out in anger:

'You'll die for this, Helot! You'll suffer, I promise!'

Lysander did not look round.

Lysander placed his mother on her bed, and looked around their shack – the few pieces of rough furniture, the cooking pans and the half-melted candles. Was this all their life amounted to? Was this all a Helot could expect?

'How can they do this to us?' No one answered. Lysander buried his face in his hands and wept. He could not hold back the tears any longer.

A fist thundered on the door. The voice of the overseer bellowed from outside.

'Open up, boy!' The hand pounded the wood again. His mother stirred, but didn't wake. *So this is it*, thought Lysander. *Six lashes will not be enough this time*. He stood, and dried his eyes with his hands, before walking to the door. He opened the wooden latch, blinking into the sunlight. The overseer stared at him, his jaw twitching and a sheen of sweat glistening on his forehead.

'I'm coming now,' said Lysander, straightening his back. 'Just let my mother sleep.' To his surprise, Agestes didn't protest. Instead, he spoke through gritted teeth.

'You will not be returning to the fields today. You have been *summoned* elsewhere.'

Dread gripped Lysander's insides.

'Summoned where?' he asked quietly.

'You are to go to the house of the Ephor Sarpedon.'

It took Lysander a moment to register the name. Then all the moisture seemed to evaporate from his throat. The old man who had saved him from the Spartan gang was an Ephor! *He cannot be!* After the two kings, the five Ephors who formed the Ephorate were the most powerful men in Sparta. Some said they were even more powerful than the two Kings themselves, because without them the Kings could not declare war. They were the ultimate guardians of Spartan law.

'An E–Ephor?' he managed to say. 'What would he want with me?' Of course, Lysander already knew. *He wants the Fire of Ares*, his mind screamed.

A smirk crept across Agestes's face.

'You had best find out,' he said. He pulled a piece of parchment out of a pocket inside his tunic, and held it out to Lysander. 'You are to take this with you. It will ensure safe passage – or so they say.'

Lysander hesitated before taking the parchment. It felt fragile in his rough hands. It was forbidden for Helots to enter the Spartan district without permission. Looking closely he saw the sheet was covered in writing. Agestes laughed.

'What? Do not pretend a dunce like you can actually read!' he said. 'You couldn't even write your own name?'

Lysander felt the blood rise to the surface of his cheeks. It was true, he could not read or write, but what Helot could? Certainly not Agestes.

'Take the western road from Amikles, then the right fork at the shrine of Apollo,' said the overseer. He stalked away. After he had gone a few paces, he turned and spoke one last time.

'See you tomorrow in the fields . . . if you are lucky!'

CHAPTER 8

The village of Amikles was about an hour's walk from the house Lysander and his mother shared. The midday sun blazed overhead. He followed the river for most of the way, which wound its way from the Taygetos Mountains to the southern sea. At this time of year, the water was low and the current hardly noticeable. By the banks, thrushes swooped, gorging themselves on insects that swarmed in the heat. Muddy islands rose in the middle of the river, too, and Lysander watched as a solitary stork paraded on its skinny legs, eyeing the shallow water for fish. Lysander had never set foot in this district before. He heard it housed only the wealthiest Spartans. There were no Helot settlements blotting the landscape here.

On the outskirts, Lysander passed the men's dining messes. These great barracks halls were where Spartan men ate, slept and trained together until they were thirty years old. Such barracks were scattered through the Spartan territories as a constant reminder of

Spartan power. As he watched, the gates of one creaked open. Two columns of red-cloaked men marched out, carrying matching glinting shields. The voice of a commander carried across the empty air.

'Phalanx positions!'

Soundlessly, the two columns each ordered themselves into four rows, several men long. The two sets of men stood facing one another, perhaps fifty paces apart. From his vantage point, Lysander could not make out their faces. The commander shouted again:

'Attack drill!'

Each group proceeded forward, first at a walking pace, then a jog, then faster still. As they drew together, both sets of men were running at full speed. They met with a crash. Lysander could see that several of the front row had fallen, but the remainder pushed on, leaning their combined weight against the opposing side, digging their heels into the ground. The thick afternoon air carried their shouts, until the side of the left began to gain the advantage. Their opponents were being shifted backwards. One by one they were turned or fell. The conquering phalanx did not stop, but simply walked over their fallen comrades. Finally, the right team collapsed entirely, and the winning squad ran straight past them. Lysander shuddered. It was hard to imagine that no bones had been broken in the brutal exercise. But Lysander was exhilarated too. As he continued on his way, the victorious chanting of the winners made his skin tingle.

The barracks faded into the distance as he reached the town itself. Passing the western side of Amikles, Lysander was surprised to see that some of the homes were not much grander than his own, but as he climbed the hill, wooden and mud walls gave way to stone. He walked by a residence with wide, columned gateways, through which he glimpsed a Helot slave, rushing with a platter of food. The streets were quiet.

Sarpedon's house was in the wealthiest area of the village. At a junction Lysander followed the right fork and soon saw the house set back from the road. His feet slowed as he gazed upwards. The building looked more like a palace than a house to him. It was two storeys tall, and gleamed white in the bright sunshine. The roof was covered in neat red tiles. A row of grapevines, laden with fruit, separated the house from the path, and his stomach rumbled.

I am about to enter the house of an Ephor – the men most hated by the Helots!

Resisting the urge to stuff his mouth with grapes, he walked towards the wide entrance. There was no door, and what he saw through the opening took his breath away: a huge, sun-filled courtyard, open to the sky, filled the central section of the house. Trees and other plants that he didn't recognise grew in pots and there was even a pond in the centre. Exotic purple flowers floated on the surface of the water. The luxury was beyond anything Lysander had ever seen. Around the edges of the yard was a shady colonnade, supported by wide, blue-and-white painted columns. Lysander spotted a girl of about his own age. She was dangling a strip of brightly coloured linen. At her feet a pet tortoise ambled, stretching its scaly neck to bite the end.

'Hello,' said Lysander, taking a few steps into the courtyard. The girl turned quickly and looked him up and down. Her dark hair was gathered loosely in a band. Her face was a long oval, a little like his own. Picking up the tortoise, she walked away without saying a word.

Lysander was left alone, and ill at ease. He noticed that the floor beneath his feet was decorated with hundreds of tiny coloured tiles, intricately arranged. As he stood back, he could see they formed the image of two horses facing each other.

'I see you're admiring my mosaic!'

Lysander looked up to see Sarpedon striding towards him. Today he was not dressed in his cloak, but a simple white toga fastened with a metal clasp at the shoulder. Lysander dropped swiftly to one knee, bowing his head.

'Rise, boy! And welcome to my house,' said Sarpedon, and then, waving his hand towards the floor, 'it is the work of a man from Rhodes. Wonderful, is it not?' Lysander was confused and didn't respond. 'Rhodes is an island across the Aegean Sea. All the most talented craftsmen come from there.'

'Yes, it must have taken a long time,' was all Lysander could manage.

'Come, sit down,' said the Ephor, gesturing to a wooden bench beside a low table.

Lysander did as he was told. *Is this really the man who seemed so terrifying last night?* he asked himself. Certainly the scars across his face didn't look so menacing in the light of day.

Sarpedon sat beside him, before calling out, 'Kassandra, please bring refreshments. Our guest must be thirsty.'

The young girl appeared at another doorway and walked over, holding a tray with two wooden cups and a terracotta jug. She placed the tray on the table and proceeded to pour the water, glaring fiercely at the cup. She would not meet his eyes. Her role fulfilled, she was gone.

'You will have to forgive my grand-daughter. She's not accustomed to waiting on Helots.' He smiled. 'Nor should she be!'

Lysander felt annoyed but also knew he could not say anything to protest. What was the point? Sarpedon was right – Spartans *did not* have to wait on Helots. He waited for Sarpedon to pick up his cup, before raising his own to his lips. The water was flavoured with mint. He gulped down the whole glass. Sarpedon poured Lysander a second cupful.

'I think you know why I have asked you here . . . Lysander,' he said. 'It took most of the morning to find you, but my messengers did a good job. Your face means that you stand out in the crowd.' Lysander's tongue felt out the tender cut on the inside of his lip. Sarpedon continued: 'Show me that jewel again.'

'I cannot,' he replied. 'It was been stolen.'

Sarpedon raised an eyebrow, and Lysander could tell that he was in no mood for games. Lysander had better go straight to the truth. It was a risk. But did he have any choice? Sarpedon could have him whipped to death if he sensed dishonesty.

'I was visiting the market at Limnae this morning. Someone put a knife to my throat and took the pendant.'

'And you didn't put up a fight?' asked Sarpedon.

'I couldn't follow the thief. He knocked me out.' Lysander lifted his hair to show the bloody mark where his head had struck the wall. The Spartan looked troubled.

'Even if it has been stolen, where did you get that jewel from?'

Lysander paused, and Sarpedon cut in, his voice raised and impatient.

'Come on, boy. I will not be deceived. You stole it, did you not?'

Lysander felt trapped, but angry. He was not a thief. *Just tell the truth,* he told himself.

'My mother gave it to me when I was born. She said it would give me strength and keep me safe. I swear to the Gods that I am telling the truth.'

'Leave the Gods out of this,' said Sarpedon sternly. 'You say the amulet was a gift from your mother. What is her name?'

Lysander dropped his head.

'She is called Athenasia,' he said.

The cup dropped out of Sarpedon's hand, rattling across the mosaics.

'And how old is your mother, Lysander?'

Lysander was not sure. 'I don't know exactly,' he said. 'Perhaps thirty-five . . .'

'And you say she's ill?' said the Spartan with a frown.

'Yes, dreadfully,' said Lysander. 'I think she may die.'

Sarpedon pushed himself to his feet, and took Lysander by both shoulders. His grip was almost painful.

'You must take me to your mother, Lysander, and you must do so immediately,' said Sarpedon. His voice left no room to quarrel. Lysander had wanted to keep his mother out of all this, but now that was impossible. He wondered for the first time where she had got the Fire of Ares. Was his mother a thief? And what would Sarpedon do with her now?

Lysander had never ridden a horse before. Sarpedon's mount, Pegasus, was a huge, hazel-coloured creature that twitched and stamped with energy. Its withers stood taller than Lysander's head. Sarpedon helped Lysander mount the horse bareback. They set off slowly, but with every jolting step, he felt himself slipping off. When they reached the path towards the settlement, Sarpedon kicked his feet into Pegasus's sides, and the horse lurched into a gallop. While his seating had been precarious before, now Lysander felt in danger of his life. He struggled desperately to grip the animal's flanks with his legs, while hanging on to Sarpedon with his hands. The dry soil burst in clouds from the horse's feet. Lysander's teeth rattled in his head as he prayed for the ordeal to be over.

He was glad when they dismounted a short walk from the Helot settlement. The Ephor, who had changed from his toga into a coarse cloak, tied the reins to a fence post.

'Show me the way,' he commanded.

When they reached the door of Lysander's home, he felt embarrassed. Sarpedon was used to luxury, and here he was on the threshold of Lysander's one-room shack. He knocked on the door.

'Who's there?' came his mother's voice.

'It's me – Lysander,' he replied, trying to disguise the worry he was feeling.

He heard the wooden bar being lifted from its cradle, and the door swung open.

'I was worried about you, Lysander,' Athenasia said, throwing her arms around Lysander's shoulders. 'They told me Agestes came here and took you. Are you all right? Are you . . .' She stopped when she spotted Sarpedon. She stumbled backwards into the room and pushed herself against the rear wall. Both hands reached for her mouth.

'How . . . no . . . why are you . . . no,' she muttered,

shaking her head. Lysander followed her in, and tried to calm her.

'Mother, it's fine. I am here,' he said, attempting to draw her hands down from her face. 'What's wrong?' But Athenasia could not take her eyes from the tall figure on her doorstep. Lysander watched as Sarpedon took three steps inside the shack, bowing his head to fit beneath the lintel. Then he spoke.

'Greetings, Athenasia. It has been a long time.'

CHAPTER 9

The Spartan Ephor stepped further into the room, filling the space around him.

'Athenasia, I mean you no harm, and I am not here to cause any trouble. I wanted only to see if it was true.'

The words had little effect on Lysander's mother. She sat, stiff with fear, her eyes wide with alarm.

'What do you want with my mother?' asked Lysander.

He had spoken louder than he intended. Sarpedon's nostrils flared and anger darted from his eyes, but just as quickly vanished.

'Shall I tell him, or would you like to, Athenasia?' Lysander's mother said nothing, so Sarpedon continued. 'Your mother and I knew each other a long time ago,' he said softly. 'Athenasia was a slave in our household for many years.' Lysander looked at his mother, who gave a tiny nod: it was true. She held out a hand to Lysander. He took it, and sat beside his mother.

'Let me tell you a story,' Sarpedon began, his deep voice comforting. 'I had two sons. Their names were Thorakis – he was the elder – and Demokrates – his younger brother. They were the most splendid young men in all of Sparta, Lysander – tall, strong, and brave. Some said they resembled Kastor and Polydeukes themselves. The Gods saw fit to take both of them in battle, the sort of death every Spartan warrior dreams of.' Sarpedon's voice became thick with emotion, but he swallowed once, and continued. 'Twelve years ago, they brought Thorakis's body back to Sparta. He had fallen to a Tegean sword, fighting on the coast. But only after he had cut down the fiercest of the enemy, a warrior called Manites. May the Gods bless him in the Underworld.'

The story set Lysander's heart thumping. Sarpedon continued.

'The younger, Demokrates, was a brave man also. He was taken from the world in his prime. Kassandra is his daughter, Lysander. He died only three years ago, facing the spears of the Elis by the western sea. My sons have both brought me honour. I wish only that I might have died before them, but I have been . . . *fortunate*.' He said the last word as though it were distasteful to him. 'They brought Demokrates back to Sparta alive, but his wounds had become infected. Before he passed to the land of the Shades, he told me something, a secret that he had long kept.' Sarpedon's eyes had become glassy. 'As he lay clinging on to life, he told me that his brother Thorakis, who was not married, had fathered a child with a . . . with a Helot woman. That woman was your mother.' Sarpedon paused and looked at Athenasia. She could not meet his eye. 'Boy,' said Sarpedon. 'Thorakis was your father.'

Lysander jumped to his feet.

'It isn't true,' he said. 'My father was a Messenian. A slave.' He looked desperately to his mother. 'Tell him, Mother,' he shouted, 'tell him it is false!'

But Athenasia kept her head bowed. Silence enveloped the room, and Lysander had all the answer he needed.

'You lied to me all this time!' he shouted. 'How could you?'

His mother did not say anything, but a sob escaped her lips. He had never raised his voice to her before. He threw his arms around her.

'I'm so sorry,' he whispered.

Lysander gripped his mother close, but his mind was reeling. *My father wasn't a Helot, he was a Spartan warrior. I'm half Spartan! Does that mean . . .?* He released his mother and turned to Sarpedon.

'Are you my —' he began.

'Yes,' interrupted the Ephor, 'I am your grandfather, Lysander.'

Lysander's mind raced. What did this mean? *Am I a Spartan, or am I a Helot? What will Timeon say when he finds out?*

Athenasia rose. 'Forgive me, I've been rude,' she said. 'I shall prepare some food. We haven't much . . .'

'That's not necessary,' said the Ephor.

'Of course it is,' she replied. 'We have some broth in the pot – I will warm it through.'

'Thank you,' said Sarpedon. He turned back to Lysander. 'After we met in the alleyway I had a strange feeling. Lying in bed, I realised what was bothering me. You see, I did not recognise the similarity straight away, but your profile was so familiar. It was like seeing my son Thorakis all over again. And now I know the truth, it is obvious.' He took hold of Lysander's shoulders and inspected his face. 'You look so alike: the same lively eyes, the strong jaw.'

Athenasia turned from the fire.

'When Demokrates returned after the Tegean conflict alone, I knew what had happened,' she said. 'Thorakis had always made it clear that a Spartan's life could be a short one. He tried to explain that death was not something he feared or avoided. He embraced the danger.' Lysander could see she was trying to fight back tears. 'But when it finally happened,' Athenasia continued, 'I was torn apart. I could not go on working in the household where your father had lived, and ran away to this settlement. I was three months' pregnant with you, Lysander.'

Sarpedon placed a hand on Athenasia's shoulder.

'I was angry that Thorakis and Demokrates went off to fight,' he said. 'Thorakis had no child to carry on the line, and Demokrates had only a daughter. But they were both brave young men, eager for their first taste of battle. Of course, I didn't know at the time . . .' and he looked at them both, '. . . that Thorakis had a son on the way.'

Lysander's mother smiled.

It was dusk outside when Sarpedon finished his broth, wiping up the remnants with a piece of bread. If it was less than the Ephor was used to, he did not comment. Placing his bowl aside, he stoked the fire with a charred stick. His face was half-lit by the flames. The afternoon had been spent telling stories of Thorakis's exploits. *My father*, thought Lysander, though the word still sounded strange. Sarpedon turned back to the fire.

'When he was twelve, Thorakis killed a wild boar with his bare hands. His mother – my wife, Jocasta – was angry that he had taken such a risk. He just had a few scrapes, but it could have been worse. He liked to pretend he was the hero Herakles, killing the vicious boar on Mount Erymanthos!'

Lysander looked at his mother. Normally she would have been asleep by this time, but she was smiling in a way he had never seen before.

'After he . . . after Thorakis was killed, his mother put all her hopes in Demokrates. But when he too died three summers ago, she could not go on. She herself passed away soon afterwards. It is too much for a woman to lose both her sons . . .' Sarpedon tailed off.

Lysander felt his grandfather's grief swell to fill the room. It was an uncomfortable silence, and he was grateful when his mother spoke up.

'After Thorakis was killed, I was afraid for you. It has been known for Spartans to expose such half-bloods along with the weak or deformed. To my surprise, Demokrates came to me with a gift – a beautiful red stone set in a golden surround.' Lysander's heart sank as he remembered the missing pendant. He saw that Sarpedon had looked up too. They met each other's eyes for a moment. *Don't tell her*, Lysander's glance said; he doubted that his mother was up to hearing that the Fire of Ares had been stolen. Athenasia carried on: 'Demokrates told me that Thorakis had wanted his son to have it. How he knew you would be a boy, I don't know, but six months later there you were, Thorakis's little son.' She shivered and yawned.

She must be exhausted, thought Lysander. Sarpedon shook himself.

'You should not be in this cold hut,' said the Ephor, rising to his feet. 'Not when you are clearly so ill. I'll arrange for proper treatment first thing in the morning – before first light. But for now I must go. It is just as dangerous for a Spartan to be caught in Helot territory as the other way around.'

Lysander had never thought of it like that before. It made him look at Sarpedon in a new light. He was no longer the stern, gnarled warrior, but an old man out after dark in a dangerous place. Planting a kiss on

Athenasia's hand, the Ephor stooped to walk under the doorframe and was gone.

Lysander remembered the secret Helot gathering of the night before, and feared for Sarpedon's safety. He strained his ears for the sound of voices. Nothing. As he set out the evening meal of bread and olives, he made a new, silent prayer to the Gods: *Keep my grandfather safe.*

CHAPTER 10

There was a light knock on the door before dawn. Lysander had hardly slept. Athenasia murmured and stirred under her blanket. Lysander opened the door hurriedly. An anxious-looking, middle-aged man stood on the threshold. He had short grey hair lying flat above a tall forehead. His tanned skin looked soft and his striking blue eyes flashed like opals in bright sunlight.

'The Ephor Sarpedon sends his greetings, Master Lysander. My name is Strabo.'

'Where is Sarpedon?' asked Lysander. 'Why didn't he come himself?'

Strabo gave a snort.

'You are still a Helot, and Sarpedon is one of the most powerful men in all of Sparta. It would not do for him to be seen around here too often. You will be lucky to share another word with Sarpedon.' Lysander felt a stab of hurt, but Strabo didn't elaborate.

'We can talk further shortly, but first I have brought

you some breakfast.' The man stepped inside, before Lysander could reply. Strabo unhooked a small sack from his shoulder and placed it on the floor. His eyes glanced around the shack. Athenasia awoke properly and sat bolt upright, staring at the stranger.

'Fear not, Mother,' said Lysander. 'This person has come from Sarpedon.'

She peered closer. 'Strabo, is that you?' she asked.

'Who else, Athenasia?' replied the man. Lysander realised they must have met before he was born.

'Do you two know each other?'

Athenasia replied: 'We did once, yes. Strabo was the head slave in Sarpedon's household when I worked there.' Lysander thought he detected a note of unease in his mother's voice.

'I was a slave,' said Strabo with slight impatience. 'But Sarpedon freed me after years of good service. I now work of my own free will. Come, let us eat. There is much to discuss.'

Opening the sack, Strabo laid out the food on a piece of coarse cloth. It was a feast: there was fresh, warm bread, bright oranges and honey-coated oatcakes. There was even some dried meat – crispy, sun-dried strips of pork. There were other items that Lysander didn't know the name of.

Lysander sank his teeth into the soft fruit – the skin was lightly furred, the flesh soft. Juice trickled down his chin. He had never tasted anything so sweet.

'What's this called?' he said through a mouthful.

87

Strabo smiled.

'It is a peach,' he replied. 'They are grown in the east.'

Soon Athenasia and Lysander were surrounded by the remnants of their breakfast. His mother had not eaten a great deal, but already Lysander saw some colour in her cheeks. Strabo had given his mother a thick, spiced medicine, and a stoppered jar containing a week's supply. Meanwhile, Lysander had gorged himself. By the time he sat back against the wall, his stomach was hurting. A loud belch escaped his lips.

'Excuse me,' he said. 'I'm not used to such rich food.'

'Indeed,' said Strabo, wiping his own lips with a square of linen.

'I had better go to the fields,' said Lysander, getting to his feet.

'How would you like never to toil in the fields again, Master Lysander?' Strabo said.

Lysander laughed, but Strabo was not smiling.

'You're not serious?' he asked.

'I am,' replied Strabo. 'From this day forward, you need never sow or reap another harvest.'

'And the River Eurotas might flow backwards up the mountains!' said Lysander. With a smile, he made towards the door.

'Wait, Master,' said Strabo. 'Sarpedon has a proposition for you.' Lysander stopped. Strabo looked at him with his piercing pale eyes.

'As you know, Sarpedon is without a male heir. But

now he has found you.' Strabo spoke as though it was a simple domestic arrangement. 'Sarpedon was wondering if you would do him the honour of entering the agoge.'

Lysander's hand dropped from the door.

'Me? Enter Spartan training?' he said in disbelief. Lysander knew all about the agoge. It was the system of education undergone by all Spartan boys in order to prepare them for manhood. It was famed for being brutal and uncompromising. Many boys did not make it, and died in the course of the training. It was the reason that Spartans had such a fearsome reputation all over Greece. If you could last the training, you could face any enemy without fear. Lysander felt his heartbeat quicken at such a prospect.

'Yes, you,' said Strabo. 'In his youth, Sarpedon was one of the greatest warriors in all of Sparta. He was a natural leader of men, and always the first to throw himself against the enemy. His sons were no different. And now it would be a great pleasure for him to see his grandson become such a man.'

'Wait,' Lysander said, 'surely I am too old. Spartans start the training when they are seven years old. I am thirteen – I've too much to learn.'

'Well, you are right that it's not normal,' said Strabo. 'But most of their training is physical, and you look strong enough from your work in the fields. You will soon catch up if you apply yourself.'

'But I am only *half* Spartan.'

'Again, it is uncommon, but it has been known for *mythokes* to enter the training.' Lysander had heard the word before – the name for children like him, born of Spartan men and Helot women. They were on the fringes of Spartan society, not truly accepted by either the master race or the Helots. Lysander looked at his mother, but her face was unreadable.

Strabo carried on:

'I have my orders – you must make the decision now,' he said.

'What about Agestes – the overseer?' asked Lysander.

'He is of no importance,' Strabo said.

'And my mother?' he asked.

'She will be taken care of,' said Strabo. 'Look, I have some errands to run for my master, and cannot waste any more time. Am I to understand you are refusing the offer?'

Things were moving so fast. Lysander could not help thinking that perhaps this was the great destiny his mother had always spoken of. His hand reached for the pendant at his neck. But of course, it was not there. His mother caught the movement.

'Lysander, where is the pendant?' The colour had drained from her face. 'Please tell me it is safe,' her voice trembled.

You fool! Lysander silently cursed himself. But before he could explain, Strabo spoke first.

'The pendant was stolen,' he said simply, with his eyes on Athenasia. 'It seems your son has trouble avoiding the more criminal elements of society.'

'Why didn't you tell me?' said Lysander's mother. 'You know how important the Fire of Ares is . . .'

Lysander started to speak.

'I didn't want to worry you. There was nothing I could have done. I was attacked at the market. Someone knew what they were looking for . . .'

'Your grandfather thinks the missing pendant might have something to do with the same boys who attacked you two nights ago,' said Strabo. 'Your best chance of recovering your property lies in the barracks. If you can find the culprit, you can get back this Fire of Ares.'

Perhaps Strabo was right.

'What about my mother?' he asked. 'You said she would be taken care of. She cannot live here without me. It would not be in Prince Kiros's nature to look after a slave who isn't earning her keep . . .'

'Don't worry about that,' she began. 'I can look after myself.'

Lysander knew she was lying. There was no chance she could make a living in her current state.

'I have orders to take her to Sarpedon's home,' said Strabo. 'She will be given a room there and the best possible medical attention.'

Athenasia let out a gasp of surprise, and Lysander turned to her excitedly. Strabo gave a smile, but it was not reflected in his eyes.

'It is the least Sarpedon can do,' he said, then added: 'So, Master Lysander, can I take your answer to him?'

Lysander would be leaving the settlement and everything he knew. Even leaving Timeon. This would be a new life, with new hardships. Another, darker thought crossed his mind. *I could use this to help the Resistance. Learn the Spartan ways. Know my enemy and teach the Helots.*

'Listen to Strabo, Lysander,' said his mother. 'This is an opportunity to escape the Helot's life, an opportunity I never thought you would have. It is rare for a half-Spartan to be accepted without a great deal of wealth. The agoge will make you into a man, and give you a life after I am gone.' There were tears in her eyes, but happiness too. Lysander turned from his mother to Strabo.

'Please tell Sarpedon I would be honoured to accept his offer.'

'There is one more thing,' said the servant. 'As a trainee, you will need a Helot to wait upon you.'

The thought disgusted Lysander. 'I won't need a slave – I have been one for long enough. No one deserves to be treated badly.'

'It is one of the regulations, Master. You do not have to beat your slave, although some boys take pleasure in doing so. Is there no one here – a friend perhaps?'

Of course, thought Lysander. *There is someone!*

'I'll bring Timeon,' he said to Strabo.

'Very good,' said Strabo. 'I will return in the morning. For now, enjoy your time with your mother.'

Strabo stood and was gone.

That evening, Lysander and his mother sat outside their hut, enjoying the last of the sun's rays. They had spoken little since Strabo left the house, and Athenasia had slept through the afternoon. Other Helots passing home from the fields gave them odd looks, but no one asked why they hadn't been in the field that day.

'Mother,' said Lysander, 'what is so special about the Fire of Ares?'

Athenasia kept looking at the sky, where the sun smeared the horizon. She pressed her lips tightly together.

'I never wanted to tell you, because the knowledge would place you in even greater danger. It belongs to a life I never thought you would share. It was your father's. And Sarpedon's before him. And his father before him. All the way back to the Trojan War, six hundred years ago. Do you know the story about King Menelaos?'

Lysander shook his head.

'Well, many hundreds of years ago, Sparta had only one king, rather than two. His name was Menelaos. His wife, Helen, was the most beautiful woman in all of Greece, but she was kidnapped by men from over the Aegean Sea, men from the city of Troy. As well as Helen, the Trojans also took all of her riches and jewels. All but this one piece. Menelaos found it on the beach from which the Trojan thieves had departed: that is how he knew they'd taken his wife. Menelaos called it the Fire of Ares, and swore on the charm that he would get Helen back. The markings on the back are in the old language. It says, *The Fire of Ares shall inflame the righteous.*

'With his brother Agamemnon, Menelaos assembled a huge fleet and sailed to Troy. They were victorious, but only after ten years of fighting. In all those ten years, the Fire of Ares kept Menelaos safe, but after the conflict Helen gave the pendant to their daughter, Hermione. It has been passed down since then.'

'Can the Fire of Ares really have survived all that time?' asked Lysander.

'Don't underestimate the power of the jewel,' his mother replied, with deadly seriousness. 'The same power that drove King Menelaos to batter down the walls of his enemy will belong to the wearer of the Fire of Ares. It represents the family – the ancestry – to which you owe your very existence. The red of the stone is your bloodline, and your tie to the past.'

Lysander *had* to recover that jewel, whatever it took. His mother reached over to him.

'I am sure you will make me very proud,' she said. She squeezed him close as the sun set.

CHAPTER 11

Lysander stood outside the barracks with Timeon and Strabo.

'And we are going in *there*?' said his friend, gazing at the building in front of them. 'They could have made it more pleasing to the eye, couldn't they?'

Lysander had to admit his friend was right. The barracks was a huge, one-storey square building built of wood. He could only see two sides, but it looked as though there was a single door in each, and a row of windows along the top, well above head height.

'Wait here,' Strabo said, then disappeared inside.

Looking at the barracks, Lysander wondered if he had made the right decision. This one building would be his home until the age of eighteen. Nearly six years! He would eat, sleep, learn and train here with other boys of his own age. *Can I really live here?* he asked himself.

'The other Helots didn't trust their ears. You! A Spartan warrior,' said Timeon. 'Agestes's face was a sight to behold.' Timeon mimicked the overseer's booming voice: '*I hope they use him for target practice.*'

Lysander burst out laughing, but had to straighten his face when Strabo came out of the barracks door accompanied by another man.

'He's bigger than Herakles!' whispered Timeon. Lysander nodded. When the two men reached them, Lysander had to lift his chin to look the stranger in the face. A thick dark beard climbed his cheeks, and one of his eyes was covered with a patch. The top half of his left ear was missing, and Lysander found it hard to keep his eyes off the ragged pink scarring.

'Lysander, this is Diokles. He's a tutor at the barracks. He will be your guide in the agoge.' Something about the way Strabo said the word *guide* made Lysander uneasy.

'So, *half-breed*,' snarled Diokles, 'you must think yourself a Spartan already.'

'I . . . ?' Lysander didn't understand.

'Well, look at your hair, boy. It hangs around your shoulders. Only Spartan warriors and women are permitted to wear their hair long. You will have to have it cut. Is this your slave?' He waved his hand towards Lysander's friend.

'His name is Timeon,' said Lysander.

Diokles struck Lysander in the chest with the heel of his hand. The blow was like a charging bull, and Lysander slid across the dirt. The tutor stood over him, his face red with fury.

'You, boy, will call me *sir*, and I will call your Helot whatever I wish. His life is worth less than yours here. Do you understand?'

Lysander was dazed and shot a look to Strabo, who stood by. Diokles leant down and took hold of Lysander's jaw, turning it so that their eyes met.

'Do.You. Understand?'

Lysander nodded.

'Y—yes, sir!'

Diokles released him.

'Follow me!' ordered the tutor, striding back towards the barracks door. Timeon helped Lysander get to his feet.

'Are you all right?' he asked.

'Yes, I think so,' replied Lysander.

Diokles was disappearing inside the barracks and Lysander and Timeon ran to catch up. Just as they reached the door, Lysander turned to say farewell to Strabo, but Sarpedon's servant was already walking away.

Inside the building it was surprisingly cool. They were in a small vestibule area, with doors leading off to the left and right. *Those must be the dormitories*, thought Lysander. Looking directly ahead, he realised that the building was not a solid square after all, but four long sides surrounding a central exercise yard.

'This way,' instructed Diokles, and led them straight ahead and into the yard. He spread his hands. 'Welcome to the arena.'

Boys filled the training ground. Immediately to his left two boys wrestled, their arms locked around each other. They circled, each looking for the advantage, grunting while their feet kicked up clouds of dust. One boy pushed a foot behind his opponent and, with a twist of the hips, threw the other boy to the floor, before landing on top. The dust stuck to the sweat on both boys' bodies.

Beyond them stood a wooden frame, hanging from which was a row of hoops of different sizes and at different heights. A queue of boys took it in turns to thrust wooden poles into each of the holes. Lysander realised it must be some type of spear practice. One boy expertly jabbed his pole several times without touching the sides of the hoops.

'Good head shots,' said Diokles. 'His brain would be on the end of your spear.'

In two lines in the centre of the yard, one row of young Spartans attacked with wooden swords, while opposite them, another row defended with circular wicker shields. They were following a pattern of pre-arranged moves, and both rows moved with precision and in symmetry. The boys shouted a count to stay in time, and the swords crashed on the shields, hard enough to shatter bones. Lysander was impressed.

More boys to the left seemed to be lifting weights in pairs. One squatted by the side of a rock as big as a watermelon. Placing his arms either side, the veins in his head stood out as he tried to lift it. Finally, with a gasp, he managed to stand straight, and place the rock on to a platform at head height. His partner then picked the rock up and ran with it to a post a few paces away, and then back again. They repeated the exercise. *Could I lift that?* wondered Lysander.

'You two, out of the way,' someone shouted, and Lysander turned to see a boy sprinting towards him at full speed. Everyone watched as the boy pushed off from the ground and sailed through the air, landing in a pit of sand.

'This is where you will do your indoor training. You will go outside for marches, and javelin and discus.'

As they worked their way through the crowd, Lysander began to understand why the Spartans were so powerful. All of their male citizens went through this. Almost every day, of every year, between the ages of seven and eighteen. Even after that, men continued to train together and live together until they were thirty. Only then were they permitted to live in a house of their own.

Timeon stood close by his side.

'It feels like being a mouse surrounded by cats.'

Lysander was about to respond when an unusual sight caught his eye. In the far corner of the yard, a boy was tied by his wrists to the top of a wooden pillar. His body hung down, so that his feet dangled above the ground. His naked torso glistened with sweat, and the muscles on his arms bulged. But the boy's face showed no emotion.

'How long has he been there, sir?' Lysander asked.

'Who?' asked Diokles, then he saw what Lysander was looking at. 'Oh, Drako, is he still there? It must be time to bring him down.' He walked behind the pillar and unhooked a rope. The boy fell to his knees on the ground.

'Thank you, sir,' he managed to say to Diokles in a deep voice. Drako got to his feet. He was heavy with muscle and as tall as Sarpedon.

'His arms are as wide as my legs!' whispered Timeon.

'Drako was caught out after dark last night – he feels the need to supplement his rations by theft. Fine, of course, but he was foolish enough to be caught. This was his punishment,' the tutor informed them. His manner was so offhand he might have been speaking about the weather.

The group they came to next seemed to be playing some sort of one-against-many game. One boy stood with his back to them as others rushed in from all sides to set upon him with their bare fists and feet.

'This is to teach a Spartan how to face several adversaries at once,' said Diokles. 'On the battlefield, you can't expect our enemy to fight one-on-one.'

The victim was quick on his feet, dodging and changing his position to meet his attackers. Each one was sent crashing to the floor or beaten back, but still they came. Lysander could see the single Spartan was getting tired. He panted for breath. Finally, one of the hunters managed to seize him around the middle and draw him to the ground. The others piled in too. *Surely they've got him now*, thought Lysander. But no! With a mighty cry, the Spartan broke free and threw the others off. He stood over them, victorious, and then walked out of the ring. But when he saw Lysander his face went deadly cold. His dark, flashing eyes, the curl of his lips and the arrogant gait were unmistakable.

Lysander reeled backwards.

'What is wrong?' asked Timeon.

'That boy,' said Lysander. 'He was the leader of the gang in the alleyway.'

'That's enough,' called out the tutor. 'Well done, Demaratos. You have proved yourself again. Your team will have extra rations this evening.' Diokles called out to everyone: 'Spartans!'

The boys ceased their activities.

'We have a new arrival.' Lysander watched the boys' eyes fall upon him, but no pair burned more fiercely than those of Demaratos. 'This is Lysander. He will be joining the barracks from today.' A murmur went through the crowd, and Demaratos raised an eyebrow. 'He will be allocated a place in the squad of Prince Leonidas, but I trust you will all give him a . . . *warm* welcome.' The other boys laughed.

Demaratos walked over. Under the single watchful eye of Diokles, Demaratos held out a hand for Lysander to shake.

'Welcome to the barracks, Lysander. If you need anything . . .' his grip tightened, crushing Lysander's fingers, '. . . anything at all, let me know.'

Lysander squeezed back, but Demaratos was too strong for him. He was grateful when the Spartan released his hand and returned to his pack of friends.

Lysander saw a fair-haired boy looking at him. He stood tall, with lean taut muscles. He approached Lysander cautiously.

'Don't let him worry you,' he said, giving a wry smile in Demaratos's direction. 'He likes to be head of the roost here.'

The boy did not address Timeon at all. It was as if Helots were invisible. Lysander wanted to talk more, but Diokles seized both him and Timeon by the elbows. They left the training area by another gateway, which opened directly into what looked like Diokles' own quarters. The tutor rummaged around in a basket to one side and pulled out a dirty red piece of material. He threw it at Lysander.

'Put this on,' he ordered. Lysander held the heavy woollen material out in front of him, and realised what it was. *My first Spartan cloak!* He wrapped the cloak over his shoulders, and attached it with a wooden clasp that Diokles handed to him. The garment was coarse and covered in dust, with a smell of sweat and mould, but Lysander did not care. He felt strange. Protected. He saw Timeon looking at him oddly.

'It will take me some time to get used to you in that,' his friend said. And then, wrinkling his nose, 'I think it needs a wash too!'

Diokles snorted. 'A Spartan boy is given a new cloak at the beginning of every year, and only one. You will train, sleep and forage in that cloak, so look after it.' Lysander looked at the grubby frayed edges of the cloak. Diokles raised his eyebrow in Timeon's direction.

'Your slave's job will be to make sure all your equipment is kept clean and tidy, and to cook your meals with the other Helots. Make sure you beat him if he fails to perform his duties to your satisfaction. Helots are naturally lazy without discipline.'

'Yes, sir!' said Lysander, but gave Timeon a smile.

Diokles pushed them both through the door, and now they were in the dormitory proper. The long room had a low ceiling, with exposed beams spanning its width, and sleeping areas spread along both walls. No one was in there now. As they walked along, Lysander noticed that each boy's area was largely the same: a simple wooden chest for belongings, a pair of leather sandals and a folded cloak, and the odd blanket as well. At the head of each low bed rested a round shield and beside it a pile of equipment. Lysander recognised a polished breastplate and some sort of hollowed-out shoulder guard. There was little to tell the sleeping areas apart, other than the occasional charm or wooden carving. *Probably to remind them of their families*, thought Lysander.

When they reached three-quarters of the way down the dormitory, there was a gap between the beds.

'This is yours,' ordered Diokles.

Lysander looked at the empty space in confusion – it was bare earth. 'Where is the bed?' he asked.

'I'm not your mother – you have to make your own here,' came Diokles' reply. 'What did you expect, a mattress made of swan feathers? We raise Spartan men here, not Athenian boys! Most of the others go down to the river and pick a few rushes to sleep on. Itchy, but at least you will keep yourself warm with scratching. Be back before the lunch bell.' He stalked away.

Lysander looked at Timeon. What had he come to?

CHAPTER 12

'I swear by the Gods that the ground shakes when Diokles walks,' said Timeon.

'I wouldn't want to cross him,' said Lysander. 'He makes Agestes look like a puppy.' Lysander and his friend stood up to their knees in the waters of the Eurotas, gathering the tops of the bulrushes. Without a knife it was difficult to break the stems, but working together they managed to steadily fill Lysander's cloak. The water was icy cold and Lysander could not feel his feet any more. But he was glad to be out of the barracks. Being confined with so many Spartans frightened him. Half his mind wondered whether or not to simply run back to the fields and his old life. But the other half was on the Fire of Ares. He did not know how he would ever find the jewel – perhaps it was not in the barracks at all. One thing was for certain, he needed as much help as he could get. It was time to tell his friend.

'Timeon,' he said. 'There is something I have been

keeping from you.'

Timeon looked up and grinned. But the smile melted away as he looked in Lysander's eyes.

'A secret?' he said seriously.

Lysander told Timeon about the Fire of Ares, about its past, and the theft. By the time he had finished, Timeon stood with his arms hanging limp by his side.

'I thought we were friends,' he said.

Lysander waded over to him, and placed a hand on his shoulder.

'We are. I'm sorry I never told you before,' said Lysander. 'But I made a promise to my mother. I did not know how important the pendant was until last night.'

'And you think it might be in the barracks?' said Timeon.

'It's possible, but I think the thief might have been dressed as a Helot. The knife was made of flint. I need you to keep your eyes and ears open for me. You are the only one I can trust.'

'I'll do what I can,' Timeon said.

In the distance they heard the clanging of the lunch bell.

'Quick,' said Lysander, scrambling to the bank, and gathering the four corners of his cloak into a knot. 'If we don't get back it could be us hanging from that pillar.'

Timeon went to arrange Lysander's bed. The dining

mess was in the back section of the barracks, and long trestle tables occupied the length of the room. Spartan boys sat along the wooden benches tucking into their food. Huge loaves of bread and shallow dishes of olives were spread out along the table, while bowls held half-melted animal fat. Not so different from a Helot's diet. The other boys tore off chunks of bread, and ate without plates. They scooped cups of water from buckets along the table. The sound of their shouting and raucous laughter filled the room. It seemed like a free-for-all.

Lysander saw a place to sit, but as he drew nearer two boys shuffled along to close the gap. No one looked at him, but he heard someone mutter, 'No room here for you, Athandros.' He walked further up the table, towards another gap. He was about to sit, when a boy placed his hand firmly in the space. 'Sorry, Athandros, this place is taken.' A few chuckles spread along the table and Lysander's face burned. Someone shouted out: 'Nowhere to sit, Athandros?' The message was clear, but why were they calling him by that name? He could not let them get to him. If there was nowhere to sit, he would eat standing up. Lysander reached on to the table to claim a piece of bread. But before he could take it, the person in front grabbed it. When the boy turned, Lysander saw that it was Demaratos.

'Sorry, Helot, you have to train to earn your food. Not splash around all morning in the river.'

Lysander made a lunge for the piece of bread, but Demaratos was too quick for him. He threw it down the table, where another boy caught it. A familiar voice rang out from further down the hall.

'Lysander! There's a space for you here.' Looking down the length of the table, Lysander saw the boy from the market the day before.

'Orpheus!' he said. The rest of the table suddenly went quiet, and Demaratos's brow creased in confusion.

'Better run away,' he said.

Lysander made his way towards Orpheus. It was a relief to see a friendly face. All eyes on the table followed his steps. Lysander slipped into the space beside Orpheus. A collective gasp escaped the other diners.

'I should have realised you'd be here,' he said. The lame boy gave a wary smile back.

'Well, I could say the same thing. I saw you this morning in the training yard.' Orpheus leant closer and whispered. 'People say you're a mothakes – is that true?'

Lysander nodded, and Orpheus cast a glance along the table.

'Well, you should be careful. Demaratos and some of the others have got it in for you; they say you should not even share the same table as a true Spartan.' He must have seen the look of concern on Lysander's face, because he added, 'Just watch your back. Here, I saved some hot food for you.' He pushed a small bowl of stew towards Lysander. 'You will need some energy for this afternoon's training.'

Lysander thanked him, then thought back to what the other boys had said to him.

'Orpheus, why did they call me Athandros?'

His friend stopped chewing, and looked down at the table. After a couple of heartbeats, his eyes returned to Lysander.

'I don't know,' he said. 'Don't dwell on it.' But Lysander could see that the Spartan's smile didn't reach his eyes. *What's he hiding from me?* Before he could ask, Orpheus changed the subject.

'Diokles put you in Prince Leonidas's squad?'

'Yes, I think so,' replied Lysander.

'That is my team, too. And if you look to your left . . .' he gestured with a piece of bread at a boy a few places along the table on the opposite side, '. . . that is Leonidas. He is the second best athlete here after Demaratos, whom you met in the yard. Leonidas's father is one of the two kings of Sparta.' Lysander gazed at the tall, pale-skinned boy. Orpheus continued, 'Of course, being a prince counts for nothing here. Anyway, he is the second son, so he cannot be king unless his brother dies.'

The groups at the table were breaking up now. Boys finished their lunch and made their way out of the hall. Lysander was hastily eating a few extra mouthfuls of lentils, when a voice boomed from above him, and a finger jabbed at his shoulder.

'How are you settling in, Athandros?' Lysander turned to see Demaratos and two companions. He recognised them from the fight in the alley: stocky, sniggering Ariston and gangly Prokles.

Orpheus used his stick to lift himself up. He was hardly an intimidating sight, but Demaratos and his gang took a step back when they saw him. A shadow of uncertainty crept across their faces.

'You are very sure of yourself, Demaratos,' said Orpheus. 'But remember that the Gods curse the proud. Apollo flayed Marsyas alive for daring to challenge him. He hung his skin from a tree.'

Demaratos and his friends backed away. Ariston tripped over a bench. When Demaratos was at a safe distance, he seemed to regain some of his cockiness.

'See you on the training ground, mythokos,' he said. Then the three of them walked away.

'I'm sure you will,' muttered Lysander.

The yard was baking in the afternoon sun, but it was the malevolent stares of the other boys that Lysander felt burning into him. Timeon had gone to help clean up the dining hall with the other Helots. At least they were ignored and anonymous here.

The boys stood lined up against the wall as Diokles paced in front of them. In his hand he held a bronze Spartan shield. It was marked with a shape like an open triangle, which Orpheus said was the Greek letter *L*, to symbolise Sparta's ancient name, Lakedaimon.

'This is a Spartan's best friend – his shield. Even if you lose your spear and sword in battle, then as long as you have your shield, you will live. When a phalanx meets its enemy, you must stand firm with this shield. It protects not just you, but the man on your left side. The only excuse for leaving your fellow warriors is death. As every Spartan mother will say to her son going to battle: "Return with your shield, or on it." Remember that, boys. I lost my eye to a cowardly mercenary archer, but I still kept in line. There is no greater shame than cowardice, and no greater honour than death.'

'Honour and death!' shouted the boys in unison, three times. On the third Lysander joined in. He enjoyed the flame of pride that flickered in his chest.

'You!' ordered Diokles, stabbing a finger towards Lysander. 'Do you think you could stand firm in a real battle?' Lysander lifted his chin.

'Yes, sir!' he shouted.

'Well, come forward,' said Diokles. 'Let us see how well you shoulder a Spartan shield.'

He stepped out of the line. *I'll show them what a Messenian can do!*

'Extend your left arm,' ordered Diokles. Lysander thrust his hand out. Close up he could see that the shield was a wide wooden dish coated in a thin layer of bronze. There were two looped wooden handles on the back: one through which to thread his left arm, the other to grip with his hand. It looked heavy, but it would not be a problem. Diokles positioned the shield and then let the full weight rest on Lysander's shoulder. With a thud the shield pulled his arm downwards and hit the floor. A roar of laughter erupted from the other Spartans, and Lysander felt like a fool.

'Silence!' bellowed Diokles, though Lysander could see he was enjoying the spectacle as much as the others. *I'll prove them wrong!* Lysander promised himself. *I am the son of Thorakis.* He focused his mind on the shield. Tensing his shoulder muscles, he heaved it from the ground. He could not help the grunt that escaped his mouth, but he managed to hold the shield aloft. His arm started shaking almost immediately, but he stared straight into Diokles' eye. It wasn't a victory, but nor was it defeat.

'Perhaps there is some hope for you,' said the tutor quietly. 'Enough.'

Lysander was grateful to put the shield down again. His arm was feather light without the burden.

'Groups of three – sword practice!' commanded Diokles. With barely a word, the boys began to order themselves, but each way Lysander looked, eyes were averted. Clearly no one wanted a new boy in their group.

'Over here,' came Orpheus's voice. Lysander saw that he was with Leonidas, and he jogged over to make up a three. At an equipment stand on the edge of the yard, Orpheus picked up a wooden shield, slightly smaller than the one Diokles had used for the demonstration and without the inlaid layer of bronze. Leonidas took a wooden sword and handed another to Lysander. He looked at the weapon, confused.

'What am I to do?' he asked.

'Why, attack me, of course,' said Orpheus.

Lysander watched as the groups around them began to fight. Swords crashed on shields, as two boys attacked each single shield bearer. It did not look like a game.

'Come on!' said Leonidas, and lunged at Orpheus, who parried the blow.

Lysander stepped forward and swung his sword slowly at Orpheus's shield.

'No, you're doing it wrong,' said Orpheus. 'You're aiming at my shield, not me! I won't have that luxury in battle.'

And so Lysander attacked again, aiming at Orpheus's chest.

'Faster,' said the lame Spartan. 'Like you're trying to hurt me . . .'

And so it went on. Lysander soon discovered that he could not have hit Orpheus even if he had wanted to. Even when he was sure one of his shots would hit its target Orpheus seemed to manoeuvre his shield into position, or flex his body out of harm's way. Soon Lysander was feigning and thrusting as fast as possible, trying to batter through Orpheus's defences. Still, not a single shot was successful, as Orpheus ducked and dodged to protect himself. He moved fluidly, despite his bad leg. Orpheus had had a lifetime of living with his lameness. It was clear that any disadvantage it might

113

once have been had disappeared. Lysander's friend was as good a fighter as anyone.

'Change over!' boomed Diokles. This time it was Lysander's turn with the shield. It was much lighter than the adult one, but still difficult to manoeuvre. Diokles watched them closely.

'If you two go easy on him, you will be punished.'

'Ready?' asked Leonidas.

'I think so,' replied Lysander.

Leonidas thrust at his chest, and Orpheus towards his legs. He dropped his shield to stop one blow, but the other hit his shoulder. He could tell they were not being as powerful as they should, but the wood still bruised.

'Faster!' ordered Diokles. 'He has to learn.'

This time the blows came harder. One hit his shin, the other his stomach. They made him angry, with both Orpheus and Leonidas, but also with himself.

'Just relax,' said Leonidas. 'Your body is so tight, you cannot move smoothly. Imagine you are like water, flowing around an object.'

Lysander tried to do what the prince suggested, and it worked a little. Orpheus's sword rang out against his shield, and Leonidas's missed altogether as he ducked to the left.

'Better,' said Orpheus.

As they fought, Lysander began to recognise when a blow was coming and in what direction by looking for little movements in his opponents' arms. Still, he was jerky and stiff, and several shots landed. Every time he blocked successfully, they congratulated him. It was slow, but he was learning. By the end of his turn, though he was dripping with sweat, he wanted to carry on.

'Good for a first attempt,' said Leonidas, shouldering his shield for his stint defending, 'but you'll hurt later.'

Lysander didn't believe him. Feeling the sword balanced in his hand, he felt he could carry on all day.

The prince was right. With dinner over and the dusk muting the colours of day, Lysander lay on his back, unable to sleep. His cloak was wrapped tightly around him, keeping the cold out at least, but the rushes hardly softened the ground at all, and every time he shifted, a new ache appeared. The angry purple bruises across his arms and thighs throbbed in the darkness, despite the lavender ointment that Timeon had found for him. A light draught fingered its way through the windows and made the room pleasantly cool. But it was not only his sore and heavy limbs that were bothering him. This was the first night he had spent away from home, and away from his mother. He wondered how she was feeling. He was grateful that Orpheus had been able to swap berths with his neighbour. It made him feel a bit safer to have an ally nearby.

Diokles called for lights out, and Lysander leant across to extinguish his candle. Now the whispering started, at first no more than a rustle in the darkness, but soon coiling like snakes around his bed. He could here snatches of conversation all around him. The voices seemed to jump around the room: 'He shouldn't be here', 'What good is a Helot going to be in battle?', 'Who is his father?' Lysander tried to block out the sounds. But then the voices started to address him.

'Are you missing your mother, Helot?'

He peered into the darkness nearby where he knew Orpheus was lying. Could he not hear the taunts? Lysander felt suffocated and afraid.

'Do not close your eyes tonight, *Athandros.*'

That name again. The voices sounded like they were all around him now, closing in, like evil spirits shifting and swirling in the blackness.

'Athandros, Athandros, Athandros.'

Lysander shot out a hand to protect himself.

'Ouch!' said Orpheus. 'What did you do that for?'

The spell was broken. The voices stopped suddenly and Lysander's eyes adjusted to the gloom. He saw his friend roll off his front and half sit up.

'Orpheus,' he hissed. 'Who is Athandros?'

The Spartan made a show of rubbing his bad leg a little as he leant close to Lysander.

'I'll tell you,' he said, 'but you must not fear.'

'I'll be fine,' replied Lysander. The other boys had tired of their bullying. One or two had even started to snore. Orpheus whispered his story in Lysander's ear.

'Athandros was another mythokos, just like you. He was in the intake above us when we joined at the age of seven. His father was one of the High Council, the twenty-eight men and the two kings who govern with the Ephors, so he could afford to send to the agoge a child he had fathered with a Helot woman, a half-breed. That was Athandros. He was a great warrior, even though many of the boys hated him. Diokles, especially, used to be tough with him. But Athandros took it all – the rough treatment only seemed to make him stronger. Until earlier this year . . .' Orpheus tailed off.

'What happened to him?'

Orpheus gave a sigh. 'When a Spartan boy reaches his sixth year of training, he must undergo a special challenge. He is sent out into the wild mountains for several days with nothing but the cloak upon his back. It is a chance to prove his worth. He has to fend for himself for those days: catching or stealing his own food, fighting the dangers of the forests and hills. After that, he is ready for the next stage of the training.'

'And?' said Lysander in the pause.

'Athandros went out but never came back. Some say he was murdered by other members of his own barracks.'

'And that is why they call me Athandros, because I am a half-Helot like him?

'Well, that's not all.' He grimaced. 'I said they didn't find Athandros. But they did find his cloak. You are wearing it.'

Fear tightened Lysander's chest, and he threw off the cloak.

'I'm sorry I had to tell you,' said Orpheus. 'Ignore their whispering. It is superstitious nonsense. Trust in the Gods, train hard, and you will be fine.' Orpheus lay back down to sleep.

The rushes from the river were itchy when not covered by the cloak, but Lysander could not bear the thought of the rough wool on his skin. Now he knew of its past, the mud stains had taken on the scent of blood. It felt like a death shroud. Perhaps he was wrong to think the Spartans had it better than the Helots! *But at least they are free*, a voice replied in his head. While Lysander's tired body dragged him towards sleep, his imagination turned over terrible images in his head. He saw Athandros, out in the cold mountains, fear gnawing his insides. What terrible thing had happened to Athandros out there? And did a similar fate await him?

CHAPTER 13

A hot slap stung the side of Lysander's face, and a sudden white flash blinded him. Instinctively, he tried to lift his head off the floor, but a rough palm pressed over his nose and mouth. He struggled to breathe as his skull was forced to the hard-packed floor. Someone was sitting across his chest, squeezing the air out of him. He tried to wriggle free but his arms were being held down firmly. He could not kick out either – his whole body was immobilised. He felt weak. Pathetic. A voice whispered in his ear, and hot, stale breath fell on his cheek:

'So, you think you can be a Spartan warrior?'

It had to be Demaratos. 'Stop struggling, and this will be over a lot quicker for all of us.' In the darkness, a blade caught the meagre light. It looked like a pair of shears used for taking the wool off sheep. Lysander writhed in fear, trying to put as much distance between the sharp blades and himself as possible. He felt as though his veins would burst, but there was no escaping. *Where was Orpheus?* Demaratos's voice was back at his ear.

'Do not fear, Lysander, we are not going to kill you in your bed. That would hardly be very noble, would it? No, consider this an introduction to Spartan life. After all, only Spartan warriors and women are allowed to grow their hair long. And you, my friend, are neither of those things. We are just going to give you a little snip.'

As the blade approached Lysander's face, he had no choice but to remain still. One wrong move and he might lose an eye, or an ear. He shut his eyes as his cheek was forced to the ground. With each slice of the blades, his hair was half cut, half tugged from his head. His stinging scalp made his eyes water.

'He's crying!' laughed Demaratos. 'He loves his hair like a woman!'

Lysander's neck was twisted as they turned him on to the other cheek. As they cut that side, he tasted the dirt of the ground on his lips. Then his head was pulled up as they sheared the back. After a final series of chops, it was over.

As quickly as they had pinned him down, his attackers melted away into the shadows. Lysander put his hand up to his head and touched his crudely hacked locks. He felt the cold air around his ears, and the vulnerable bones of his skull. He curled into a ball, and instinctively his hands reached for his chest, for the pendant that was his source of courage and comfort.

Not there. He asked himself: *Would I have been able to fight Demaratos off if the Fire of Ares still hung from my neck? Would I have lifted the shield with ease?* Perhaps. Ever since the amulet had gone missing, his strength seemed to have abandoned him.

After a long time, the cold forced him to wrap himself in the dead boy's cloak.

'Wake up!' The tutor bashed together a ladle and a tin pot. 'Enjoy this lifetime, it's the only one the Gods have given you!'

As the boys sat up in bed, eyes swollen with sleep and hair ruffled, Timeon came into the room with the rest of the Helots. Some carried clean training clothes, others pieces of equipment or small items of food. The Spartans took their offerings without a word of thanks. Timeon handed a smock to Lysander.

'Here, my mother washed some of your old farming clothes for you. They should be fine for training in.' Lysander thanked him. 'What happened to your hair?' Timeon asked, with a puzzled expression.

'Demaratos,' replied Lysander. Timeon seemed about to say something, but then merely nodded.

Lysander climbed out of bed, and threw off his cloak, picking up the tunic that Timeon had brought along. From across the room, he saw Demaratos staring at him.

Demaratos tapped Ariston on the shoulder and pointed in Lysander's direction. He spoke loudly, so

121

that everyone could hear.

'Well, well, perhaps there's more to this half-breed than meets the eye. Not such a skinny runt as I expected. Still, big muscles will not get you far unless you know how to use them.' Demaratos picked up a wooden sword from the end of his bed. The whole room had fallen silent, and they stopped their dressing as the Spartan approached Lysander, all the time swinging the sword in dizzying arcs. He found Diokles' words hammering in his head: *Stand firm. Stand firm. Stand firm.* The sword was a foot's length from his face, now a hand's width. Still he stood with his feet planted to the floor. The wood was a blur and he could feel the air swishing past the tip of his nose. Then in walked Diokles. Demaratos lowered the sword.

Diokles snatched the sword from Demaratos's hand. He motioned the sword at Lysander's throat.

'Are you making our newcomer welcome?' he hissed, fixing his eyes on Lysander. 'I'm sure you all know by now that Lysander here is not all he seems.' A murmur rippled through the spectators. 'I don't know why he is here, either. All a Helot is good for is making a Spartan's breakfast or cleaning the latrines, but this half-breed seems to have friends in high places. *They* seem to think he can make it in the agoge, but *I* have serious doubts about that.' He pushed the tip of the sword into Lysander's sternum, catching him off balance. Lysander fell backwards on to the floor. He felt like a fool, writhing in the dirt.

'Just as I thought,' chortled Diokles. 'A pushover!' He turned to the other boys. 'Not fit to polish a Spartan shield.'

'I'm as good as any Spartan,' Lysander said to Diokles' back. Diokles turned around. He grabbed Lysander's smock and lifted him off the floor. Lysander felt Diokles' knuckles digging into his chest. The tutor brought his face up close to Lysander's.

'What did you say, Helot?' Lysander flinched as spittle peppered his face. Lysander was dragged outside, stumbling and half-running across the ground. Diokles hurled Lysander to the dirt and the other boys gathered, excited, in a circle around both him and the tutor. The only sound was the clanking from a nearby mill-wheel. Lysander caught sight of Orpheus's face in the crowd and looked at him pleadingly. But Orpheus gave a small shake of his head.

Diokles' face was almost black with fury, and he shouted his words from the depths of his belly. 'Better than any Spartan, are you? Better than any of these boys?' he pointed around the circle. 'These boys have spent five years training for their manhood. Five years of hardship, pain, endurance. Cold nights of hunger and fear. And what have you achieved? You have grown up in your mother's bosom, enjoying life in the fields. You have no idea about what it takes to be a Spartan. But I am here to show you . . .'

The crowd jeered, as Diokles dragged Lysander to the edge of the circle. A gap opened up to let them through. Diokles pushed Lysander straight over to a millwheel, where two yoked oxen were slowly pushing the wooden arm in a circle, driving the central axle. A Helot stood idly by with a whip, ready to keep the beasts moving if they stopped for a break. Diokles strode over and took the whip away from the Helot. He then detached the harness from one of the oxen and with a crack of the whip sent the animal plodding to one side, its eyes rolling in its head.

'The time has come for you to learn the meaning of endurance, half-breed. You Helots are no better than animals. Worse, in fact, because at least they do not answer back. Today you are going to do the work of an animal, so start pushing.'

Lysander looked at the wooden arm, and then at Diokles. Was he serious? Diokles swung the whip and it lashed against Lysander's back with a crack. The pain was sudden and unexpected, and Lysander was ashamed to hear himself cry out.

'Get to it, boy, or I will whip you till you cannot wail any more!'

Lysander hurried forward and placed both arms on the wooden beam of the millwheel. He pushed with all his strength, but nothing happened; the axle did not budge.

'Harder!' bawled Diokles.

Again, Lysander strained with his muscles, until his palms ached and his pulse was thumping. Still, the mechanism did not move. He may as well have been trying to move a mountain. *I need the Fire of Ares!*

'One more chance, boy, then you're mine,' said Diokles. Lysander could see that the tutor's fingers were white from tightly gripping the whip. Lysander had been whipped many times in his life already. He could well imagine the bite of the whip's leather across his back.

Lysander dug his heels into the dust and summoned all his energy. He offered a prayer to the goddess sacred to farming and the fields: *Please, Demeter, give me strength!* Then he gritted his teeth and pushed.

The ox on the other side of the axle let out a low moan, and Lysander sensed the arm give a little. He carried on heaving. The arm moved more. *Keep pushing!* The axle started to creak, and Lysander found he could take a step forward. Then another. Then one more. '*Thank you!*' he whispered, both to the goddess and to the ox opposite, whose head bobbed up and down in time with its steps. His own feet shuffled at first, his calf muscles tight, his kneecaps threatening to burst, but gradually his steps grew wider. *I can do this!* he thought. To his amazement, a small cheer went up from some of the Spartan boys, and despite the burning in his arms and legs, Lysander experienced a hint of pride. Soon, the millwheel was turned slowly, but fluidly.

He completed the first circuit and met Diokles' eyes as he came around. The tutor gave a snort, then handed the whip back to the Helot.

'If he stops before the lunch bell, whip him as hard

as you can.' Then he turned to the students. 'What are you gawping at? Back inside!'

The sun licked Lysander's shoulders like flames as the wheel slowly turned. He had no idea what time it was, though he could tell that the sun had risen high in the sky. He followed his shadow on the ground beneath his feet, unable to glance up. His legs screamed in agony, and the muscles in his arms felt stretched and torn. *Sarpedon, where are you? I need your help. I cannot do this . . .*

A noise hovered on the edge of his thoughts. Clanging dully, repetitively.

I want to go back home, to see my mother, I want to work in the fields and laugh with Timeon.

The noise again. What was it?

Lysander sank to his knees in the dust and collapsed face first to the ground.

Something cool touched his lips. *Water!*

'Lysander . . . Lysander!' said Timeon's voice. 'The lunch bell.'

Lysander rolled on to his back and allowed the cool water to splash over his face. Above him, the sun shone down harshly. His lips were cracked and he could barely open his mouth to speak.

'I did it,' Lysander whispered, as Timeon gently raised his friend's head on to his lap.

'You did.' Timeon smiled, wiping the sweat from Lysander's brow. 'You did it.'

CHAPTER 14

As Lysander entered the dining hall for breakfast, every muscle was a ball of pain. Yesterday, the other students had seen him being carried into his barracks by Timeon. A slave carrying a boy-in-training! But no one had jeered. Boys had even bowed their heads respectfully as Lysander passed them. But as soon as Timeon put him down on the bed of rushes, Lysander had fallen into a deep, dreamless sleep. He had woken only when the spasms from his muscles forced him to reach for the jar of water that Timeon had left in arm's reach.

Now Lysander took his place beside Orpheus at one of the benches.

'How are you feeling?' asked the Spartan.

'I've felt better,' replied Lysander. He felt older – like a different boy to the one who had entered the barracks as a Helot slave.

Orpheus nodded. 'You know, don't you, why I could not help you yesterday? Why I had to stand and watch with the others?'

Lysander looked up from his bread and goats' milk. Orpheus looked serious.

'You probably thought Diokles was singling you out yesterday, bullying you. But we have all been through the same. The agoge does not leave any room for kindness, or compassion. We are here to become Spartan warriors. Diokles was testing you. One day, you will be on the battlefield, maybe with Diokles at your side – he wants to make sure you are ready.'

Lysander listened carefully to Orpheus, but he wasn't so sure. His friend hadn't seen the look of hatred in Diokles' eye.

'Anyway,' said Orpheus, 'we have academic lessons this morning. Your arms will get a rest.'

That was just the news Lysander wanted to hear. He stood up and called over to Timeon, who was standing with the other Helots at the end of the hall. Timeon hurried over and bent his ear to Lysander's mouth.

'Quick,' said Lysander. 'We don't have long.'

Lysander made sure there was no one in the dormitory.

'Stay by the door,' he whispered to Timeon. 'If anyone comes, let me know.'

'Of course,' replied his friend. 'Where do you think it will be?'

Lysander cast his eyes around the room. Could his pendant be here somewhere? The dormitory only had so many hiding places. There were perhaps eighty beds, all surrounded by personal items. He went to

Demaratos's first, running his hands over the rushes that made his sleeping mat, and under his feather-stuffed pillow. Nothing. His eyes fell on the embossed chest that stood by Demaratos's bed. He did not feel brave enough to look in there, not yet.

Next he went to Prokles' bed, then Ariston's. But the Fire of Ares wasn't in either. The chest beckoned to him. Could he risk it?

Timeon coughed by the door, and Lysander rushed over to his own bed. Ariston entered the room, suspicion playing around his eyes.

Lysander addressed Timeon.

'Slave, what have you done with my sandals? Find them by this evening, or I will give you a beating you will not forget.'

'Yes, master,' said Timeon, hiding his smile from Ariston, before rushing out.

'Time for lessons, half-breed,' said Ariston to Lysander with a sneer. 'Do not be late.'

The schoolroom was shared by several barracks, and was located a short walk away past the central well. As they passed, a group of Helots were heaving up buckets of water, and carrying them in a line to the dormitory. Leading them was Demaratos's slave, Boas. He was a big, dark-skinned boy, perhaps a couple of years older than Lysander and the others. As they passed, Prokles stuck out a foot and tripped him. Boas crashed to the floor on his face, and the water sloshed out of his buckets, running across the dry earth.

'Better watch your step, slave,' said Prokles, standing over the fallen Helot. Boas looked up, but did not say anything. His forehead and cheek were streaked with dirt, and his face glowed red. Lysander read the frustration in the slave's eyes, and his knuckles cracked as he clenched his fists. Lysander strode towards Prokles, imagining hurling the cheap coward to the ground. A hand on his arm steadied him.

'It's not your fight, any more,' said Orpheus in his ear. 'You are going to have to learn to be a Spartan now.' Lysander hesitated, then let his friend gently pull him away. They walked to the school hut.

The schoolroom was a shack half open to the elements. The lower part of the walls was made of wood, and the roof of overlapping palm leaves was supported on a timber frame.

'I don't know why we are here at all,' grumbled Demaratos, as he sat on the floor. 'We are Spartans, not scholars. What use are poems facing an Athenian in battle?'

'Demaratos . . .' A tall, thin man stepped into the doorway, wearing a coarse brown toga. 'Sometimes the muscle you have in here . . .' he tapped his shiny, bald head, '. . . is more important than the muscles in your spear-arm.' A smile spread across his face, revealing dazzling white teeth. He did not look like a Greek to Lysander. His skin was dark, and his eyebrows rose in thin arches. His face was kind, and his eyes twinkled like quartz in the sunlight.

'That's Anu,' whispered Orpheus. 'He is our teacher. He comes from across the Great Sea, from a land ruled by the Sun God, whom they call the Pharaoh.'

Lysander looked at the eagle-eyed teacher. 'Why is he here?' he asked.

'He came to Sparta before we were born, to learn about our people, but he decided to stay. People say he is the wisest man in all of Greece. He has hundreds of scrolls filled with writing from around the world, and he can speak five languages!'

'I want you to recite the poem we learnt last time,' said Anu. He began to sing in a soft, low voice: 'What is better than when a brave man . . .'

The rest of the class joined in, but Lysander didn't know the words. He could only listen.

What is better than when a brave man
Falls and dies in the front ranks for Sparta?
What is worse than when a man runs away
And is left begging with his poor mother,
Aging father, little children and loyal wife.

The beauty of the words stirred Lysander's heart. He thought of the future, and of his mother. He wanted to make her proud, to make Thorakis proud too, the father he'd never met. *This is my destiny.* He could hear Orpheus's voice above the others, clear and melodic:

131

He will be despised wherever he goes,
Reduced to nothing but rags and hunger.
Shame will follow his ancestors always.
Scorn and misery will sniff at him like dogs.

But a man is at his best when young.
He looks his finest dying in the forward clash.
Let each man root his feet on the ground,
Bite his teeth into his lips, and hold.

The class fell silent. The final words rang out in Lysander's head. *I must get through this! I must bite my lips and hold on.*

'Very good,' said Anu. 'Tyrtaios would be proud.'

Without thinking, Lysander said out loud, 'Who is Tyrtaios?'

The class erupted in laughter, and Lysander blushed.

'Silence!' said Anu, and gave Lysander a steely look. 'You've only recently joined us? Tell him, somebody, who was Tyrtaios?'

Demaratos answered.

'He was a great Spartan poet. He lived over one hundred years ago, and led our people to victory in battle when they smashed the Messenians during the last Helot war.'

Lysander's heart missed a beat at the name of his countrymen. He had heard stories about the wars between his people and the Spartans, but they were all shrouded in legend.

'Tyrtaios showed that a poet could also be a great soldier . . .' Anu continued.

'Unlike Terpander,' interrupted a voice from the front.

'Do not interrupt, Hilarion,' said Anu, 'unless you have something useful to say. What do you know about the great Terpander?'

Hilarion, a talkative boy whom Lysander thought more friendly than most of the others, answered, 'Well, sir, Terpander was giving a recital of his poetry at a festival competition. He won, and someone in the crowd threw him a fig. He ate it . . . and choked to death!'

Hilarion and the rest of the class started guffawing, but Anu frowned and shook his head.

'That's enough!' he said, and the laughter ceased. 'You shouldn't believe such foolish rumours. Terpander lived to the age of eighty-four and died tending his vineyard.'

The topic changed to the law, and the edicts of Lykurgos, the founder of Sparta. Lysander listened intently as the class recited his teachings. He learnt that Lykurgos had created the Ephorate and the Council of Elders to help the kings govern. It was he who had created the agoge and enslaved the Helots. Though he lived more than three hundred years ago, he had shaped almost every part of Lysander's life. Lysander felt himself shiver involuntarily.

'The final part of the lesson will be given to writing,'

proclaimed Anu. A groan went around the classroom.

'We didn't do this when Diokles was in charge of classes,' Demaratos grumbled. 'He said writing was for those who could not hold a spear.'

Anu responded with a shake of the head.

'The Council of Elders has decided all children must learn to write. When a Spartan goes into battle, his cloak is fastened with a piece of wood that bears his name. That way, after the fight is over, the pieces of wood can be collected from fallen comrades to identify who has been killed. Think, Demaratos, if you cannot write your own name, your family might think you have run away from the fight. Once you have all managed to write your names then we'll finish for the morning.'

Anu took out a shallow wooden board, with raised edges. It was covered with a milky, slightly shiny layer of wax. The board went around the classroom as Lysander looked on nervously. Each boy took the sharpened wooden stylus and scratched his name into the wax. By the time it came to Lysander, the last in the class, his hands were sweaty. He looked at the markings in the wax – they meant nothing to him. His hand hovered above the board. The stylus felt unnatural in his grip.

Around him the rest of the class was getting restless, until someone shouted the words he'd been dreading.

'The half-breed cannot write!' Lysander looked up to see the other boys staring at him. He lowered the stylus and gouged a line in the wax, but Orpheus snatched the wax tablet out of Lysander's hands, and held it up.

'Yes he can, you idiots. Look!' He pointed to some markings in the wax and grinned at Lysander. 'There, below my own name. It says *Lysander*.'

The cat-calling died down and Lysander looked too. Though he could not understand the shapes etched into the waxy surface, he knew that Orpheus must have written his name as well.

Thank you, he mouthed to his friend.

Anu took the board back and surveyed the signatures.

'Right, class dismissed. And by the way, *Aristos*, our new boy's spelling is much better than yours!'

'Pay no attention to them,' Orpheus said as he joined Lysander by the well. The day was hot and all the students were helping themselves to a drink. Demaratos was at the front of the queue, drawing water from a bucket. 'They will tire of it and find someone else to harass. Just stand up for yourself.'

'They don't seem tired yet, though,' said Lysander.

'Demaratos and his gang used to make fun of me for my bad leg,' replied Orpheus, cupping water into his mouth. 'We are not so different, you and I. Both victims of our birth. Easy targets.'

Demaratos stepped between the two of them. Orpheus struggled to keep his balance against the edge of the well. A quick look around confirmed that Lysander was surrounded on all sides: Demaratos, Ariston, Prokles, Meleager. Four pairs of eyes nailed him to the spot. Demaratos wiped his dripping mouth on a sleeve.

'You think you're a Spartan because you can write your name, do you?' He did not give Lysander time to reply. 'Well, don't get above yourself just yet. Yours will be the first name-tag they find on the battlefield. If you even make it that far.'

'That doesn't frighten me,' replied Lysander. 'After all, first to die means first in honour. Unless you fear to lead the phalanx.' A few boys laughed and Demaratos shot a look around him.

'Are you calling me a *coward*?' asked Demaratos slowly.

'I am just saying what I see,' said Lysander.

Demaratos's hands were around his throat, and he was thrown off balance, leaning over the edge of the well. He scrambled to get a grip, but he was helpless, at Demaratos's mercy. His stomach tightened with fear. Over Demaratos's arm, he could see Orpheus hobble forward. Ariston blocked his path.

'Hold back, cripple.'

Orpheus looked on – his mouth open in silent astonishment. Lysander struggled, trying to prise Demaratos's fingers away. They were like iron claws. Demaratos leant further over, pushing more of Lysander's weight over the lip of the well. He could feel the abyss below him, the emptiness tugging him down. He stopped struggling. He was completely at Demaratos's mercy. The Spartan was all that stood between safety and the long drop.

How deep is the water? he wondered. *Could I survive the fall?*

'So, who is afraid now?' spat the Spartan, the veins in his forehead standing out. 'You should not be here, Helot. You cannot make it as one of us. Your sort are born to hold a rake or a brush, not a spear. No one will care if you take a tumble.'

'Do it, Demaratos!' came Prokles' voice. 'We have had our fill of this impostor.'

'Yes, drop him,' echoed Ariston. 'We'll say it was an accident.'

Demaratos turned back to Lysander. His jaw flexed and his eyes looked cold as a hawk's.

'The Underworld awaits you, Helot.'

Demaratos let go. Lysander felt weightless for a moment, and then gravity pulled at his shoulders. Panic shot through his chest like lightning, and his head fell first into the blackness. There was nothing he could do to stop himself falling, and he heard his own screams echo off the well.

CHAPTER 15

Pain shot through his ankle and his breath caught in his chest. He had stopped falling. A hand gripped his foot tightly and hauled him slowly out of the well's mouth. Lysander landed in a heap on the ground, gasping for breath. As the blood rushed back out of his head, he saw that Demaratos was standing well back, his face pale and afraid. Lysander's rescuer was Diokles, who stood with his hands on his hips, breathing heavily. Diokles looked from Lysander to Demaratos and back again, his mouth twitching beneath the shadow of his stubble. He seized hold of an arm of each of them and marched off, dragging them with him. All the other boys followed, like a pack of dogs, whispering to each other. Lysander didn't know what to expect.

When they reached the training square Diokles stopped.

'If you are going to fight,' he bellowed, 'you will do so properly.'

With the sword from his belt he scraped a circle on

the ground, with a radius perhaps four times Lysander's height. Lysander felt dread gathering in his belly.

'You!' Diokles pointed at Demaratos and then in the centre of the circle. 'You need a taste of your own medicine,' he shouted as Demaratos made his way towards the middle.

'But he deserved it,' protested Demaratos. 'He said –'

'No excuses,' interrupted the tutor. 'One against many!' Diokles stalked towards the crowd of students, and quickly pulled out five boys. 'You know the rules. Go!'

Lysander watched as the boys quickly entered the circle and surrounded Demaratos, who dropped to a crouch. Suddenly he looked alert, powerful. His arms were spread, ready to take on attackers from all sides. Lysander realised that 'one against many' must be a form of wrestling. The first boy darted forward, but Demaratos was too quick for him. He grabbed the boy's foot and lifted it high in the air, sending the boy sprawling back out of the circle. Two more boys came in from opposite sides. Demaratos rolled smoothly out of their midst and repositioned himself so that one was blocking the other's path. He dealt with them one at a time, the first with a powerful punch to the leg which dropped the boy to the floor with a howl of pain, the second by ducking under a swinging arm and lunging at the boy's chest with all his body weight. The opponent crashed to the floor with a sickening thud. The final two did not look at all confident stepping up against Demaratos. He took one down by sweeping his legs away, and the next by an elbow to the chin. A spray of blood spattered the ground. Lysander could not believe the ruthless efficiency of his enemy.

'Very good, Demaratos, very good.' Diokles clapped slowly, before turning to the attackers, who lay about rubbing their sore bodies. 'You five, clean yourselves up.' Then he pointed his sword at Lysander. 'You next, half-breed. You need to practise looking after yourself.'

'But I have never wrestled before,' protested Lysander.

'Well, this will be your first lesson,' said Diokles.

He nodded to Ariston, who dashed back into the barracks complex.

Lysander waited in the centre of the circle, and Ariston came back out carrying a wooden rod as long as his arm.

'To make things a little more interesting . . .' said Diokles. Up close Lysander saw that the rod had some sort of twine attached to each end, which Diokles tied around Lysander's ankles so that the rod rested between his legs. It meant that his feet were positioned at a set distance apart, and moving comfortably was very difficult. Another five boys were selected.

'That isn't fair,' said Lysander. 'I don't stand a chance!'

'Painful lessons are always the easiest to learn,' shot back Diokles. He spoke to the five on the edge of the ring. 'Teach him.'

Lysander tried to mimic what Demaratos had done, crouching low and turning quickly to face each side, but the wooden bar meant he could only take clumsy steps, and he could not use his feet to fight back. He sent the first boy flying with a dizzying cuff to the ear. The others fanned out, and they began to dart in and out, testing Lysander's reactions. Anger tightened in his sinews.

'Come on, you cowards,' he said, casting a sneer, and gesturing with his hands. He saw the boy in front nod to one behind, as he stepped within range. Only as he swung his fist did Lysander realise it was a feint. The attacker ducked and Lysander felt pressure on his ankles as the wooden rod was yanked away by the boy behind him. Lysander saw the ground rush towards his face and threw out his arms to protect himself. At the same time, a knee crashed in his temple. Then, black.

Cool water moistened Lysander's dry tongue. He opened his eyes, squinting in the light. Someone was holding a cup to his mouth. A trickle escaped over his lower cheek. As he shifted slightly on to his elbows, a dull ache spread across the right side of his head and his stomach churned. He started to choke as water filled his throat.

'Take it slowly.' came Timeon's voice.

His friend was sitting over him, wearing a concerned expression.

'I didn't win the one-against-many?' asked Lysander.

He attempted a weak grin but the pain in his head made him wince.

'No, and if you don't come quickly, you will miss lunch.'

Despite his protesting head, Lysander climbed to his feet and accompanied Timeon to the dining hall.

Ariston and Prokles sniggered as Lysander walked past them in the dining hall.

'Are you hungry?' jeered Demaratos. 'Not full after eating all that dust?'

Lysander ignored them, and none of the other boys seemed to take any notice of him. He supposed someone getting knocked unconscious was nothing special in the agoge. Prince Leonidas did give him a small nod, though. Towards the end of the meal, there was a banging at the far end of the table. Lysander saw Diokles standing with his arms folded.

'Silence, students,' he called out. 'The Council of Elders has announced the date of the Festival Games in honour of the Goddess Artemis Ortheia, Protector of the Young. They will take place in thirty days' time, on the night of the full moon.

'Each of the two squads must nominate ten boys to represent them in the athletics competition. Demaratos will lead one squad, Leonidas will command his. First you will all have to wrestle a boy from the other team. If you win you go through to round two – the javelin. Here the five furthest throws will progress to the final:

the foot race. Quickest over two lengths of the stadium is the winner of the competition. Train hard and do not let me down. Good luck, boys!'

The whole room erupted in a cheer, but Lysander kept his eyes on his plate. He wanted to prove himself, but the task seemed impossible. There were over a hundred boys in the barracks and only twenty places. Over the last few days he'd been battered, starved, bruised and scorched by the sun. His strength had vanished and the passion that had once driven him was cold and dormant. The memory of the Fire of Ares gleamed red and burned in his mind's eye.

'Have cheer,' said Orpheus from beside him. 'The Festival is the most exciting time of the year. It can make a boy famous for the rest of his life.'

'I won't even get in the team,' said Lysander.

'Not with that attitude,' replied Orpheus. He put a hand on Lysander's back. 'You need to put your faith in the Goddess Artemis Ortheia; she'll guide you to victory.'

Lysander wasn't so sure. 'I haven't seen much evidence of the Gods lately!'

'That's because you aren't looking hard enough,' said Orpheus. 'You've a great deal to give thanks for. Without the Gods, Demaratos might have pushed you down that well.'

'It was Diokles' hand that stopped me falling, not the Gods',' said Lysander.

'Perhaps,' said Orpheus, rising from his seat, 'they are the same thing.'

It was javelin practice straight after lunch, and Lysander was dreading it. He had never even held a javelin before. He came out of the dormitory, where he had concealed a couple of oranges to give to Timeon later on. He found the barracks students queuing behind the dormitory huts by a wooden rack that held around ten javelins. Lysander joined the back of the queue.

Diokles stood in front of them, by a line he had drawn on the ground. He scanned the row of boys.

'Leonidas, you will be first.'

The prince stepped forward, and took a javelin from the rack. It was not as large as a Spartan spear – the shaft was shorter and thinner. Around the middle was tied a piece of leather. Lysander followed closely, as Leonidas threaded his index and middle fingers into the two loops of the leather thong. He steadied himself, then took five steps and launched the javelin. Lysander watched as the shaft spun and sailed through the air. For a long time it seemed to hang horizontal before the tip dipped. Then it thudded into the ground just a few paces beyond the well.

'Very good,' said Diokles. 'Lysander, you are next.'

'But I haven't –' he began.

'No excuses!' bellowed the tutor.

Lysander did as he was told, and lifted one of the javelins from the rack. He tried to do the same as Leonidas and placed his fingers in the thong. But it didn't feel natural. The shaft didn't balance well on his hand.

'Hurry up!' said Diokles.

Lysander stepped to the line, and drew back his arm. He concentrated all his power in his shoulder, as he brought it forward. But as he was about to release it, he heard Demaratos behind him.

'Take care you do not throw it in the well, *Helot.*'

His concentration was broken. Something went wrong. He tripped. The point snagged in his clothing. A loud rip, and the javelin left his hand at an angle, clattering to the ground a few feet away. A raucous laugh burst from the Spartans behind him, and he scrambled to his feet to see them doubled over. He looked at his torn tunic, which hung off his body.

'Get inside and get changed,' ordered Diokles.

Lysander's cheeks burned with shame and he hurried inside.

In the cool, still air of the dormitory, Lysander let his heartbeat steady. He had been humiliated again, and felt utterly worthless. How would he ever compete with these boys? How could he hope to match them without the Fire of Ares?

He darted over to the doorway and quickly glanced out. The javelin practice had resumed. He might have a little while longer before they came looking for him. He crept over towards Demaratos's sleeping area. It must be in his chest.

145

He knelt on the floor and ran his fingers over the rim. A bead of sweat broke out on his forehead as he lifted the lid. He opened the chest, and delved inside. Nothing but a few carved figurines, a scrap of parchment, a golden belt clasp, and some clothes.

Lysander stood up, and kicked the box in anger. Pain shot up his toe, and he fell to the ground. He sat there furiously rubbing his foot, and cursing himself. *I am so stupid. I'll never find it.*

Then he noticed that the chest had moved slightly. There was something unusual about the ground beneath it – a space. Suddenly the pain in his foot vanished, and he leant over to inspect the hiding place. Lysander pushed the heavy chest further aside. A hole about a foot wide and half a foot deep had been excavated from the soil, and in it was a smaller, simply carved wooden box. Lysander lifted it slowly out, and brushed the loose earth off the top.

This must be it! This must be the Fire of Ares. Lysander could almost feel the pendant calling to him.

He opened the lid.

His heart plummeted like a stone in a well. The box was empty but for a piece of fine linen embroidered with a word. Lysander's reading was coming slowly, but he could make out the letters: DEMARATOS. Delicate red flowers were stitched around the name.

A love token! He didn't think Demaratos was the sort. He had been so sure that his enemy had the amulet.

146

A noise outside made Lysander jump. He crossed the room quickly to his own bed, and pulled his torn tunic over his head as Hilarion came in.

'Diokles wants you outside right away,' he said.

Lysander threw on clean clothes and ran outside.

Diokles was waiting, javelin in hand.

'Throwing the javelin is not just about distance, it is about aim too. There is no use throwing your spear at the enemy if you are more likely to hit one of your own men. So now we are going to do some target practice.'

He hoisted his javelin aloft and hurled it through the air. It landed between the barracks and the schoolroom. Lysander felt anxiety gnawing at his insides, but he hoped he would be able to acquit himself better this time.

Diokles shielded his eyes with a hand, and peered at where his javelin had fallen.

'I cannot see where it landed,' he said. 'Lysander, go and stand by it.'

Lysander did not know what the tutor was up to, but he ran over to the javelin. It was about a hundred paces away. When he got there, he turned and looked back to where Diokles and the students were standing.

'Stay right there,' shouted Diokles, before turning to the others. 'Boys, you have your target.'

CHAPTER 16

'But –' Lysander started to speak.

'Stop your Helot tongue!' yelled Diokles. 'Or I shall come over there and tear it out of your head! If you want to be a Spartan, you have to show courage. On the battlefield, when the spears and arrows of the enemy are raining on you like hail, you cannot simply run away. You have to stand firm by the men at your side.' He pointed to the boys in front of him. 'Show him no mercy. If your javelin falls further than ten paces from him, I'll hang you upside down by your legs until the blood leaks from your ears. Do you hear?'

The students looked at Diokles, and then at each other. No one spoke.

'I said, do you hear me?' spat Diokles.

'Yes, sir,' said the students hesitantly.

'Good,' said Diokles. 'If any boy hits him, I shall personally donate a roasted suckling pig for your supper. Leonidas, you are first.'

Lysander didn't know what to do. He felt his legs

shaking, and locked his knees together. Should he run? If so, he doubted Diokles would hesitate to spear him.

Leonidas stepped forward with his javelin. Even at this distance, Lysander could see there was no expression in his eyes. He pleaded mentally to the prince, with his lips moving silently: *Please don't do it!*

But Leonidas did. As the javelin left his hand, Lysander fought the instinct to close his eyes. His insides tightened as he stood transfixed. The javelin seemed to move in slow motion until it reached the top of its arc, then descended with terrifying speed. It landed about six feet away, thumping in the earth. The shaft wobbled for a few moments and then was still. Lysander felt his muscles relax.

'Who wants to go next?' asked Diokles.

'I will,' said a voice, and Prokles grabbed a spear.

What a coward! thought Lysander. *I'd like to see him roast over a fire like a pig.*

Prokles lined up and launched the javelin, but he threw it too hard, and it landed well behind Lysander. The Spartan kicked a foot in the dust and Lysander allowed himself a sigh of relief. But he knew the trial was not over.

'Don't look at the javelin,' said Diokles. 'Look at where you are throwing it.'

'My turn,' cried Demaratos, striding over to the javelin stand.

Lysander watched him test the weight of one of the spears, then replace it. He seized a second. This one seemed to be more to Demaratos's liking. He took his time adjusting his fingers in the straps and then lifted his head, staring straight at Lysander.

He took four long, slow paces back from the throwing line, lifting the javelin to shoulder height.

He paused.

He stepped forward and threw.

As soon as the javelin left his hand, Lysander could see he was in trouble. It glided perfectly straight, and then began its descent as a single dark point in the sky. Lysander's whole body seemed to become light, and he hardly felt attached to the ground any longer. This time he did close his eyes, and imagined the sharp tip hammering into his chest, sinking through his soft flesh and bursting through his back.

He heard a low thrum, and then a *thwack!*

He opened his eyes. The shaft of the javelin was touching his arm, vibrating still. The point was buried in the ground less than a finger's length from his foot. For the first time in his life, he was sure of the Gods.

'It is important that every Spartan soldier is able to endure long marches into enemy territory,' barked Diokles later that day. Lysander stood outside with the others by the front gateway of the barracks. 'So this afternoon we will be strengthening your legs. We are going to run to the outskirts of the free-dweller settlements and back again, and we shall do so in formation. Assemble yourselves!'

The clouds had gathered and dulled throughout the morning. Now the sky was a leaden grey. Lysander followed as best he could at the rear of the ordered rows and columns of boys. Orpheus, he noticed, stood to one side, leaning on his stick. Clearly he was excused these forced marches. All the other students were barefoot, in order to toughen the soles of their feet.

'If any boy falls behind, he will be made to carry additional weight on his back. There is no place for weaklings in –' Diokles was distracted by a figure approaching slowly on a donkey. As the rider came closer, Lysander recognised him. *Strabo!* After Strabo dismounted, he and Diokles spoke briefly, both flashing glances in the direction of the gathered students. Diokles turned to them.

'Lysander, step out!' he bellowed. A murmur rippled through the crowd and Lysander walked to the front, ignoring the mutterings of those around him.

'Lysander, you are excused to go with this slave,' he said.

As Lysander walked along the line, Demaratos hissed:

'But come back soon, Helot.'

The journey with Strabo took place in silence and Lysander was grateful to climb off the uncomfortable donkey. He rushed into the courtyard, just as the first drops of rain began to spatter on the mosaic floor.

Sarpedon was knelt at one side by a smoking tripod. His head was dipped and his lips moved in silent prayer. Lysander waited patiently under the sheltered portico, wondering which of the Gods of Olympus his grandfather was speaking to. The rain fell more heavily, hammering the roof. It lifted the scent of flowers to Lysander's nose.

When Sarpedon had finished, he turned to Lysander and smiled.

'Greetings, my grandson,' he said, striding over and stepping between the columns. He offered his arm in formal greeting, and Lysander took it.

'Greetings,' replied Lysander. 'Is my mother well?'

'She is a little better,' said Sarpedon. 'I have sent a maid to tend to her until she feels strong enough to make the journey. If all goes well, she should be here by nightfall.'

'Thank you,' said Lysander. He dared to hope that she would all right.

'Tell me, boy, it is your third day in the barracks. How is your training progressing?'

Lysander was embarrassed. *Can I tell him how much I hate it?* He could not even meet the Ephor's gaze.

'What is wrong, Lysander? I know Spartans do not like to waste their words, but I asked you a simple question. How goes life in the agoge?'

'Badly,' replied Lysander, tracing the mosaic floor with his eyes. 'The tutor is a bully. He seems to enjoy beating me at every opportunity, and putting me in humiliating situations. He hates the fact I'm a Helot, and treats me like I should not be there. The other boys follow his lead. I cannot sleep at night because of the whispering.' Lysander wanted to tell his grandfather everything. Perhaps he could help? 'And it is all because I haven't got the Fire of Ares. I do not have the strength to continue. Every day is harder than the one before . . .' He looked up, expecting to see sympathy in the old man's face. Instead, anger furrowed the older man's brow.

'Well, what did you expect?' said Sarpedon coldly. 'This is not a soft school of Athens. This is Sparta.' Sarpedon stood to his full height and turned away, walking into the courtyard. Rain quickly darkened his cloak, and plastered his hair across his forehead, but Sarpedon didn't seem to notice. Lysander was reminded of the stranger he had met that first time in the dark alleyway by the slaughterhouse. The Ephor breathed slowly and faced Lysander again. Rivulets coursed down his face. The anger had drained from his features and he looked pained.

'Have you understood nothing? Boys have been through the same thing as you for generations. I endured it myself. Once I was beaten so hard by my tutor that I could not walk for a week. What you single out as unfair punishment, we call education. Any Helot would bless the Gods for what you have: a chance to escape slavery. A chance to be somebody the future will remember.'

Lysander felt shame flood him, prickling up under his skin. He dropped to one knee. 'I apologise,' he said.

'I will not disappoint you again.'

'This is not about displeasing me,' said Sarpedon, his voice inflamed with passion. He came back towards Lysander, and pulled him up roughly. Lysander was locked in his grandfather's stare. 'This is about you, and your father. You have a chance to make Thorakis proud, and to continue his family name. The Fire of Ares comes second to that; it is the heart that beats beneath it that will get you through. Spartan blood flows through it – a warrior's blood. The amulet is a symbol, a stone, little more.'

The Ephor's deep voice resounded in Lysander's ears, and each word seemed to build on the previous one to make him feel strong. *Perhaps I can get through the agoge. After all, I am still alive now. I just have to take one day at a time.*

'I have another proposition,' Sarpedon said. 'I'd like you to come here for some additional training before the Festival. Each morning, be here as the sun rises. Can you do that for me?'

'Will Diokles allow it?' asked Lysander.

'It is doubtful,' Sarpedon replied. 'I could force him, but it would be unwise to draw further attention to your case. No, you must come in secret. Stealth is also part of a Spartan's training. Slip out and make sure that no one sees you. Understood?'

'I will do my best,' said Lysander. 'Thank you.' His grandfather's grip softened and he pulled Lysander towards him in a hug.

154

'You have great strength in your heart,' said Sarpedon, 'and the blood of Thorakis flows in your veins.'

The words fired Lysander with new hope. He wanted to be the best, to make Sarpedon proud. He was ready to find the Fire of Ares, and to prove himself a warrior. Their dawn lessons would be the first step towards that. They would tread the path together.

CHAPTER 17

Lysander awoke from unsettled sleep early, his stomach fluttering with nerves. He sat up and let his eyes get used to the darkness. The other boys all lay still, and their steady breathing was the only sound. It was now or never. He stood up slowly, tying on his sandals in silence. Taking care to watch where his feet fell, Lysander tiptoed towards the exit. He was just three feet away when Prokles, his grubby feet protruding from the end of his cloak, grunted and turned over. Lysander froze. But Prokles' eyes didn't open, and his mouth was slack in sleep. Lysander slipped through the door.

Outside, the air was chill and moist, and Lysander was glad of his ragged cloak. He was now fully awake. Rain had fallen during the night, and he splashed though puddles. Through the thick cloud, the full moon was nothing but a smudge of pallid light. As Lysander descended into the centre of Amikles, haunting wisps of mist drifted at ground level. He tore through them, imagining he held a sword that slashed his enemies aside. Despite the cold and wet, Lysander felt more alive than ever as he made his way along the deserted streets. It felt like the dawn of a new era. In the solitude, there was no one to threaten him as a Helot, or cast doubt on him as a Spartan warrior. He felt free to be anything he wanted. He reached Sarpedon's doorway without meeting a soul – Spartan, free-dweller or Helot.

In the courtyard, a fine layer of condensation made the marble glisten and the floor was slippery. Sarpedon emerged to meet him, wrapped in a thick, woollen cloak.

'Good morning, Lysander. I trust your journey was without incident?'

'Yes, thank you,' he replied.

'Part of the Festival Games will involve throwing a javelin. Have you much experience with a spear?'

'Only one lesson,' he admitted, remembering the previous day's embarrassment. Sarpedon looked disappointed.

'Well,' said the Ephor, 'spears are for thrusting into the enemy line. Throwing should be a last resort, as you are then giving your weapon to the other side. So before you can learn to throw, you need a strong arm and good balance.'

Sarpedon walked over between two columns and took hold of a spear that was leaning against the wall. It was much longer than the javelins they had thrown at the barracks. The shaft was at least two heads taller than Sarpedon himself, but not much thicker than the javelin. It was perfectly straight and looked slender but deadly. The old man handled it with ease. Lysander had never seen such a weapon close up. At one end was a narrow, tapered bronze head, and the other end was a wider, heavy spike.

'The shaft is made of ash wood, which is rare in this part of the world. Though it feels light, it will bend a good deal before snapping, and flies through the air smoothly.' Sarpedon hoisted the spear aloft in a smooth movement, his fingers shifting their grip to balance the weight. He stabbed it forward in an underarm thrust, and closed one eye, gazing along the perfectly straight shaft. The tip did not wobble in the old man's grip. 'The spearhead is used for thrusting into your enemy. You see the ridges from the point?' Lysander nodded. 'They are to let the blood escape. The heavier end – we call it a "lizard sticker" – is for finishing him off as he lies on the ground. When you get to the battlefield for the first time, you will learn that a man does not often die quickly, and sometimes you have to help him on his way. The lizard sticker also helps balance the spear for throwing.

'When fighting in the phalanx alongside fellow Spartans, you can either thrust the spear over-arm, aiming for your enemy's head, neck or chest, or under-arm, going for the groin and stomach.' Sarpedon demonstrated both actions with a firm lunge. Lysander winced to think of facing the Ephor, even now, in battle. 'It depends on how the other soldiers are holding their shields. I took this spear from a Tegean in the years just after Thorakis was born. He managed to stab me right through the thigh, shattering the bone.' Sarpedon pulled back a fold of his tunic. There, on the outside of his leg, and indented into the flesh above his knee, was a pale, puckered scar.

'How did you survive?' Lysander asked.

'I pulled it out and put it through his chest,' replied the Ephor.

Lysander looked at his grandfather's face. It was easy to imagine him thirty years before in his prime, raging on the battlefield. What must it be like to face such a man in the fury of the fight? Lysander looked at the spear in a new light. *This weapon has actually taken someone's life; perhaps it has even been used to kill a Spartan!* He pictured Sarpedon tugging it out of his own torn flesh, and then using all his weight to drive it through a gap between shield and body. The point breaking through the resistance of armour and skin, perhaps the crack of ribs, blood coursing down the shaft.

'You try,' said Sarpedon, and tossed it to Lysander, who lurched forward and caught it. The spear was not heavy and fitted comfortably into his hand. Lysander felt powerful. The spear was lethal, but it was beautiful too.

'Right,' said Sarpedon, 'hold the spear high above

your head, keeping it horizontal.' Lysander lifted the shaft to above shoulder height, and found his hand naturally sat two thirds of the way along from the head. He wondered how far he'd be able to throw the weapon. 'Now, stand on just your left leg, and put your right out behind you.' As Lysander did what he was told, he found his right arm, holding the spear, rotated forward to retain his balance. Now the shaft was vertical and its weight, no longer balanced, pulled his arm downwards towards the ground.

'Very good,' said Sarpedon, nodding his head. He walked away to the door at the far end of the court-yard. When he reached it, he turned and said, 'Hold that position until I come back. Do not let either your right foot or the spear touch the ground.'

Then he was gone.

The sun had come up and Lysander saw that the roof-tiles above were catching the first of the day's rays. Though the sheltered courtyard was still in the shade, Lysander's forehead streamed with sweat and he could see the condensation misting off his body.

He was not sure how long Sarpedon had been gone, but it seemed like an age. His standing leg was trembling uncontrollably and he struggled to control his breathing. Panic was fighting its way in – what if he slipped and fell on the slick marble floor? He would have failed. He kept his eyes focused on the tip of the spear, which hovered just a few finger widths off the floor. His shoulder burned, and he longed for nothing more than to let his burden rest on the ground. He wondered if the old man was watching somewhere from the shadows. 'I can do this,' Lysander said through gritted teeth. He heard footsteps behind him. *Thank the Gods*, he thought.

But it was not the Ephor. From his right emerged the young girl – Sarpedon's grand-daughter – Kassandra. She was wearing a pale violet tunic, and her blue eyes rested intently on him. She walked around him in a slow circuit, her steps light on the stone floor. Lysander strained to look over his shoulder and saw her smile. There was no pity in her gaze, only amusement. Finally, she spoke.

'You seem to be struggling, slave-boy. Perhaps you shouldn't be playing with a Spartan's weapons.'

Lysander said nothing. He had no energy for arguments. He focused again on the spear tip. Kassandra leant in closer and pushed down gently with a fingertip on Lysander's extended right arm. Pain screamed through his muscle at even this lightest of touches.

'Does that hurt?' she asked. Lysander screwed his eyes and managed to keep the arm steady.

There was a clapping from the far end of the garden.

'That is enough, Kassandra,' said Sarpedon, walking back out. 'You can rest now, Lysander.' As the girl backed away, Lysander let the spear clatter to the ground and he fell to his knees. For a few moments, he sat on the floor, rubbing his sore shoulder. When he looked up, Kassandra was gone.

'Well done, Lysander! You didn't give up. That is the Spartan way.' Sarpedon offered a hand, which Lysander gratefully took. He was hoisted to his feet. 'As a reward,' Sarpedon went on, 'perhaps you would like to visit Athenasia?'

The name shot through his brain, erasing the pain in his limbs in an instant. *My mother!*

'Is she here?' he asked. 'Now?'

'Yes, come this way,' said the Ephor. For the first time that day, Sarpedon seemed more like his grandfather than a Spartan noble.

It was still dark in the bedchamber where Athenasia lay, and Sarpedon lit a candle before leaving the room. Lysander carried the cup of hot, honeyed milk to his mother's bedside. At first she seemed confused to be woken, but familiarity soon smoothed the lines of her face.

'My son!' she exclaimed.

Lysander could see that she was still thin and ill, but the darkness beneath her eyes was almost gone. She was getting proper rest in Sarpedon's care.

'Do I not get a hug?' she asked, pulling herself upright. Lysander put down the cup and bent over his mother, taking her bony shoulders in his arms and burying his head in the space between her neck and collarbone. He could not help the tears that stung his eyes.

'Don't crush me,' she laughed. 'You aren't wrestling now.'

Lysander released her and sat on the edge of the bed, wiping his eyes.

'You look . . . stronger,' he said, smoothing the blankets.

'I'm in good hands,' she said. 'Your grandfather is busy, but he visits me every day. And if the weather is clear, Sarpedon's maid takes me into the courtyard. It's so nice to be in the sunshine without Agestes's barking orders.' She paused. 'Tell me about school.'

Lysander looked at the flickering candle flame for a moment, then at his mother's face. There was no way he could tell her the truth.

'Well, it's hard. Not like the fields, but I go to bed every night exhausted. There are endless drills with swords and shields, or wrestling.' He tried to think of positives. 'I am learning to read as well.'

'Ha!' exclaimed his mother. 'A Helot learning to read! Bless the Gods.'

'The food is good,' said Lysander. 'We have meat or fish almost every day, and the bread is fresh.'

'Are you looking after Timeon?' asked his mother.

'It is more like he is looking after me,' said Lysander, forcing a smile. 'But I always save a bit of food for him – most of the other boys treat their Helots badly, or act as though they are not present at all.'

His mother nodded slowly.

'And the Fire of Ares?' She squeezed his arm. 'Have

you found it yet?'

'No, not yet,' replied Lysander. He decided to lie. 'But I am close, I know it.'

His mother took a long draught of the milk, and lay back. Her eyelids were drooping once again. Lysander left her to sleep. He left the room in high spirits. Sarpedon was nowhere to be seen. There was not time to say farewell, and he set off for the gateway.

As he left the villa, something caught his eye further down the street. Lysander crept back behind the grapevines so that he could watch unobserved. Two figures, leaning close together. He could tell by the purple of her clothing that one of the figures was Kassandra. She stood at a distance, beneath a twisted olive tree. The person she was talking to had his back to Lysander. He wore a black tunic. They stood like conspirators, their heads close. Then the young man was gone, marching swiftly in the opposite direction. Kassandra stared after him for a moment, then began to stroll slowly back to the villa. She looked deep in thought.

Lysander stepped out from the shade of the vines. He waited for Kassandra to spot him. Lysander could just hear the small intake of breath as their eyes met. A muscle twitched in her cheek. But then, quickly, she raised her chin and looked past him. Invisible. She behaved as though he simply wasn't there. *I will not let her get the better of me again*, thought Lysander. He took a step closer, completely blocking her way.

'Why are you so horrible?' asked Lysander quietly. 'I've done nothing to deserve it.'

'I do not know what you are speaking of,' she replied, but he could see a flush had risen in her cheeks. Lysander was so close he could see the flecks of green in her hazel eyes. She blinked her long dark lashes. He noticed how symmetrical her features were. Even the freckles on her face seemed evenly distributed. Her face was proud like Sarpedon's. There was only one imperfection, a pale scar in the arch of her left eyebrow.

'Of course you do,' he said, raising his voice slightly. He was gratified to see her slightly taken aback. 'You seem to enjoy taunting me for no good reason. Were you born like that, or do they tutor Spartan girls in the art of cruelty.'

'How dare *you* speak to *me* about Spartan women? You need to learn your place, slave, or I shall tell my grandfather what you have said. I don't know why you are here, but I shall find out and put a stop to it.' She pushed firmly at his chest, and he stumbled backwards. She turned into the villa.

Lysander was ravenous. After his dawn meeting with Sarpedon and a full day's training, he was ready for his evening meal. The Helots had laid the table as usual, with loaves of bread, fresh fruit and bowls of broth. He sent Timeon back for seconds and then thirds. He gave his last bowl to Timeon, as always. The Helot attendants were not officially allowed anything but the leftovers from the Spartan table, or what was dropped on the floor: unripe olives, the gristle from meat, pieces of burnt or stale bread. Timeon was already looking a little meatier around the face, now that so much of his day was spent at the barracks rather than in the fields.

His friend returned from washing the plates and bowls.

'I'll see you tomorrow, then,' he said.

'Wait,' said Lysander, taking out a large lump of cheese from under his folded cloak. He handed it to his friend. 'There, that is for your family,' he said, 'courtesy of Sparta.'

Timeon smiled, but then frowned.

'That's stealing. You should be careful –'

'Don't worry,' Lysander cut in. 'Spartans say there is nothing wrong with stealing. It is the getting caught you have to avoid. Diokles told us a story about a Spartan boy who once caught a fox. He planned to kill it and eat it. But when he noticed some soldiers coming, he hid the animal under his cloak. Even though it chewed and clawed his stomach open, he did not grimace or make a sound until the soldiers had passed.'

Timeon wrinkled his nose in disgust.

'What happened to him?'

'Diokles said he died, but died a true Spartan.'

Timeon did not look convinced.

'Well, a cheese shouldn't do you much harm

compared with that!' he smiled.

They walked to the entrance of the barracks.

'Until tomorrow, then,' said Timeon. Lysander did not want his friend to go – he felt suddenly homesick.

'Wait,' said Lysander. 'Do they talk about me back at the settlement?'

Timeon's gaze fell to the ground for a moment.

'Of course they do,' he said eventually. 'Of course. Messenia has not had a champion for decades. My sister says you will be the next Polykares. First, the Festival Games, next the Olympics . . .'

'Anyone other than your sister?' said Lysander.

Timeon's face looked strained.

'Lysander, do not fear, we are all behind you. Even if –'

'Even if . . . what?' interrupted Lysander.

Timeon smiled.

'Even if nothing,' he said. 'Sleep well.'

Lysander leant against the door as the darkness swallowed his departing friend. What had Timeon been afraid to say? Had his countrymen forgotten that he was one of them? In his heart he still felt like a Helot, but perhaps the cloak on his shoulders was more than just a source of warmth. Maybe it made them afraid.

CHAPTER 18

Sarpedon greeted Lysander with a formal handshake in the courtyard.

'Are you ready for today's lesson?' he asked gravely. He was holding what looked like a torn strip of clothing in one hand. A full-size Spartan shield hung from the other arm.

'Yes . . . I'm ready,' Lysander replied.

'Then take hold of this.' He handed Lysander the shield.

Lysander did as he was told, threading his arm through the grips. The weight dragged at his arm, but he steadied his feet and tried not to grimace. Sarpedon had a further surprise for him. Without saying a word, he placed the material over Lysander's eyes and tied it behind his head. Lysander stumbled in panic as his world went black.

'In battle,' Sarpedon intoned deeply, 'a Spartan is not one man, but many. Just as he depends on the shield of the man to the right of him to offer protection in the phalanx, he must in turn provide cover for the man on his left. Without this trust, the phalanx collapses and the battle is lost. Do you understand?'

Lysander nodded.

'Good,' continued Sarpedon. Lysander realised that his grandfather had changed position, and turned his head to locate him. As Sarpedon continued talking, his disembodied voice circled Lysander. 'In the heat of the fight, with blood and sweat coursing down your face, you will effectively be fighting blind. You will have to trust in the skills you have learnt and trust in those fighting with you. Today you will learn to fight blind. Literally. Are you prepared?'

'What are you going to do?' Lysander asked. He was furious with himself for feeling so frightened. How could a simple blindfold knock his confidence like this? But he was determined to see this thing through.

'You will find out all in good time,' said the old man.

There was a swish of air, and something like a cane smacked against Lysander's shin. Not very hard, but enough to sting.

'Ouch!' he yelped.

Sarpedon did not apologise. 'You just lost your leg below the knee.'

'But how am I supposed to defend myself if I cannot see?' asked Lysander.

'A bat cannot see as it plucks insects from the night sky,' replied Sarpedon, 'but it does not go hungry. You must feel your surroundings. We will continue.'

This time Lysander heard Sarpedon move slightly in front of him and he adjusted himself accordingly. Again, there was a swish, and he lifted his shield. The cane caught on the rim and deflected softly on to his shoulder.

'Good!' said Sarpedon. 'A flesh wound only.'

He heard his grandfather move quickly to his right and a brush of air. Lysander bent his left knee and lifted his shield above his head. The cane crashed into the middle of his shield.

'Excellent,' said Sarpedon. 'You fight well for a bleeding, one-legged warrior!'

Lysander felt pride swell within him, and the shield felt lighter on his arm.

They carried on. Lysander stopped concentrating on the blackness that enveloped his eyes, and instead listened for the movements of Sarpedon and anticipated where he would strike next. Soon, only one in five blows were landing on his body, and in time, none at all.

As Lysander pulled the blindfold away, his arm ached as though it was about to fall off, but he was happy. He felt more responsive to his surroundings and had discovered new ways to manoeuvre his body. Strength was important, but it was not everything a warrior needed. He would need his wits as well.

Sarpedon returned with a pomegranate and a jug of water. He took out a knife and cut into the skin of the fruit, exposing the ruby red flesh beneath. It reminded Lysander of the missing jewel.

'I'm beginning to think that the Fire of Ares isn't at the barracks,' he said.

Sarpedon gave a small grunt of interest and handed over a piece of the fruit.

'You must keep looking,' he said, biting into his own fruit.

'I have searched everywhere I can think of,' continued Lysander.

His grandfather's eyes were on him, but the gaze was unfocused. Then Sarpedon looked away, his brow furrowed. Lysander could not understand why his grandfather was so uninterested. The Fire of Ares was the thing that had brought them together. Had he forgotten that?

'Did I do something wrong?' asked Lysander.

Sarpedon passed a hand over his face, smoothing the frown away.

'What? . . . No, of course not, my boy. The Council of Elders is meeting today with the kings and the Ephors. There are important matters to be discussed.'

'What matters?' asked Lysander. He felt as though he was being held at arm's length.

Sarpedon stood up and shook his head.

'It is not the time to talk about such things.' He picked up the shield and started to make his way back towards the house. 'You should go,' he said over his shoulder. 'Tomorrow, yes?'

Lysander watched his grandfather walk inside. 'Goodbye,' he said to no one but himself. Where was the man who had taken him by the shoulders and proclaimed he saw the face of Thorakis?

A voice interrupted his thoughts.

'I know what you are thinking, Master Lysander.' It was Strabo – he must have sneaked in from outside. 'But remember: once a Spartan always a Spartan. Family always comes second to the State. You will always be below Sparta in his heart.'

Lysander didn't want to talk to Strabo, and he was annoyed that the servant seemed to be able to read his mind.

'I must leave –' he said.

'Just one thing,' Strabo interrupted. 'I wanted to ask if you had been successful in your search for the pendant. What is it called now? The Fire of . . .'

'Ares,' Lysander told him. 'The Fire of Ares. No, I have not.'

Strabo looked away, then gave a crooked smile. Lysander felt a sudden, strong urge to get away from this man.

'Maybe I will go and see my mother,' he said.

'Oh no, you must not,' said Strabo, guiding Lysander by the elbow towards the gateway. 'She needs her rest. Leave her for now.' He gave a glance in the direction of the bedchamber, then turned back to Lysander. 'Well, good day to you. I am sure you will find the Fire of Ares soon.'

★   ★   ★

172

After eating as much as possible for breakfast, Lysander stood from the bench, stuffed some bread under his cloak to give to Timeon later, and dashed out to join the other boys in the training yard. He slammed right into someone, and cold water splashed on to his feet. He felt a twinge of anger, but then saw who he had crashed into: Boas. The big slave stood trembling, holding a bucket in each hand. He must have come from the well.

'I am sorry, Master Lysander,' he mumbled, falling to his knee. 'I did not see you there. Please do not tell Demaratos, I beg you.' Lysander realised he had never heard Boas speak before. Just another anonymous Helot slave.

'Don't be silly,' he said, waving a hand at his feet. 'It's only water.'

Boas looked confused, and stood up again.

'Thank you,' he said, nodding quickly before making off towards the dormitory. Lysander remembered briefly what Orpheus had said about accidents of birth. *In my old life,* he thought, *we might have been friends.*

In the yard, Diokles stood in front of all the other boys. They huddled close together, looking at the ground. Diokles' face was purple with anger.

'I have been informed that one of you has been outside the barracks in curfew hours.'

Lysander felt a chill creep up his spine.

Did someone see me? he panicked. *They could not have. I was so careful.*

'You all know the rules,' continued Diokles. 'And you all know the punishment if you break them.'

Lysander swallowed, but his throat was dry. He was afraid, but he also felt disappointed in himself – he had let Sarpedon down.

'That person was Drako,' said the tutor.

Lysander breathed out slowly, willing his heartbeat to slow down.

'He was caught stealing food once again, this time from a bakery. Drako, step out!' ordered Diokles.

Silently, Drako presented himself in front of the tutor. They were almost the same height; the Spartan boy walked with a defeated stoop, looking warily at Diokles.

'Take your position by the flogging post,' said Diokles, pointing.

Without a word, Drako shuffled over to the wooden post where he had been hanging that first day Lysander had come to the barracks. He put his arms around it. He obviously knew what was expected of him. Diokles walked behind him and unravelled the short whip from his belt.

'The normal punishment for breaking the curfew is twenty lashes, but Drako has shown repeated disregard for those rules. So today he will receive . . . one hundred strokes.'

The boys in the crowd gasped and there was a shuffling of feet. Drako broke his silence.

'Sir, you cannot . . . not a hundred,' he choked. 'No

one can take a hundred.'

'You will take what I give you, boy,' thundered Diokles. He gathered himself, rolling his shoulders and giving a few practice swings of the whip against a doorframe. Drako heard the crack and rested his head against the post. His face was pale. His voice was little more than a quaver when he next spoke.

'Sir, please tell me one thing,' he said. 'Who told you I was outside?'

'That is none of your business,' replied Diokles. 'Now turn around.'

The first blow fell between Drako's shoulders, but he did not make a sound. Lysander pitied him. He could imagine the searing pain, making his legs weak at the knees. Diokles continued, landing stroke after stroke. Drako took the first thirty well, with nothing more than the occasional grunt. Then the blood started to appear through his tunic. First a spot or two, beading from the lacerations on his back, but after fifty, his clothing was sodden with blood. With each blow, he let out a moan, too weak to shout in pain. Still Diokles did not relent. The tutor was now making more noise himself, grunting with the effort, his face red and sweating. His blows were wilder, some hitting Drako's neck, others the backs of his legs. By seventy, the clothing on Drako's back had started to shred away, and Lysander could not watch any more. There was no hiding from the terrible sound of the whip, though. Lysander counted the last thirty blows, watching the bowed faces of the other boys. Some still watched, but he could see their faces twitching in horror with every blow. His own behaviour flashed across his mind, sneaking out of school each morning. How many lashes would that be worth? *How many could I take?* He felt sympathy tug at his stomach, but there was a stronger feeling: relief. At least that was not his shredded back.

When the hundredth lash was counted, only then did Lysander look up.

Drako was no longer standing. He was on his knees, breathing shallowly, but most of his body weight was supported on his shoulder, which leant against the bloody pillar. There was no skin on his back at all, just pink flesh and half-clotted blood. His clothes were nothing but tatters gathered loosely around his body, and the ground beneath him was stained dark.

Diokles threw down the whip and wiped the sweat from his brow with his forearm. His whole body was shaking.

'Clean him up,' he said. Then he strolled out of the training yard.

CHAPTER 19

Lysander had checked every bed in the dormitory for the pendant, but with no success. He had almost given up hope. Nevertheless, time passed quickly. At the barracks, Demaratos and his cronies continued to torment Lysander, but he concentrated on training for the Festival Games. Even without the Fire of Ares, he was determined to succeed. There had been no sign of Drako since the day of the flogging. Some said that he was being cared for by his mother and sisters outside the barracks, a shameful way to live. Lysander could not believe a boy had nearly been killed just for letting his hunger get the better of him. A few boys grumbled that the food rations were not enough to keep them strong, but Lysander found the broth, loaded with shreds of meat and chunks of vegetables, much better than he was used to. He always spared some for Timeon, too.

In some ways, his days as a Spartan were not so different from his life as a Helot. Instead of working in the fields for Agestes, he trained in the barracks for

Diokles. Both were hard, bullying masters. Where before he had secretly crept to the millhouse before dark, now he slipped out to Sarpedon's villa for extra tuition. But the similarities ended there. His grandfather exercised his mind as well as his muscles, teaching him about philosophy and history. Where Diokles used orders and fear, his grandfather used encouragement and questions.

Injuries were common as the competition became fiercer for the honour to represent each squad. A boy broke his ankle in a one-against-many, and Lysander badly twisted his wrist throwing the javelin.

The morning after his injury, he rose from his bed stiff and in pain. He walked to his grandfather's, cradling his forearm. As he trained, Lysander noticed how gloomy Sarpedon seemed to be. They had finished a leg-strengthening lesson, and Lysander sat with his back cooling against a column as Sarpedon mixed a poultice for his wrist in a dish over a tripod. Without turning round Sarpedon began to speak.

'This will be our final lesson for some time.'

The words took Lysander by surprise. He had come to rely on these morning tutorials.

'Why?' he asked, trying to keep his voice calm. His grandfather stopped mixing the ingredients and laid out a bandage.

'Because war is coming,' he finally said. 'War with Argos.'

Lysander was confused. He thought Sparta was at

peace with the Argives. 'But why does that mean we have to stop our training?'

Sarpedon spooned out brown sludge from the dish and on to the bandage. 'Because,' he replied, 'when Sparta goes to war, one king stays in the homeland, and the other leads the country to battle. The laws state that he must be accompanied by two Ephors. That is what my meetings have been about. Ten days ago the Council of Elders sent a messenger to the Oracle at Delphi.'

Like all Greeks, Lysander knew about the Oracle. It was the most sacred place in the world, where the prophets of Apollo told the future in riddles.

'The Oracle told us that we must kill the mother snake before she bears her children.'

'But what does that mean?' asked Lysander. 'You have to fight?'

'Do not fear, boy,' said his grandfather, 'I will not be in danger – I'm too old to hold a shield and spear in battle. I will leave that to better men than me. But Spartan law must be obeyed. I have been selected to follow King Cleomenes to the north. If we do not take action now, the Argives threaten to arm the Helots, and that cannot be allowed to happen.'

Arm the Helots, thought Lysander. He thought back to Cato, dead in the fields, and old Nestor with his midnight gatherings. Now he had seen first hand the ruthless barracks training of the Spartans, the brave Helot plans for revolution seemed naive and misguided. They had no idea what they were up against. 'But surely the Helots are not a threat to Sparta. They are just farmers, labourers . . .'

Sarpedon gave a hollow laugh and picked up the bandage.

'Hold out your arm.'

Lysander extended his painful wrist. His grandfather carefully placed the bandage underneath. He wrapped one side around Lysander's thumb, then again over his wrist. The heat from the brown mixture was instantly comforting. It was fascinating to watch Sarpedon's huge, scarred hands perform such a delicate operation. He wrapped the bandage around several times before tying it off. He then looked hard at Lysander, and sighed deeply.

'Tell me, how many Spartan soldiers live in the five villages and all of the lands ruled by the two kings?'

'Um, I . . . don't know,' replied Lysander.

'Well, I shall tell you, honestly. The number stands at about thirty thousand. All trained in the art of war. Now, how many Helot men of fighting age do you think there are? In all the fields and villages under Spartan control?

'The answer is *three hundred* thousand. All trained in the art of farming, building and other crafts. Not fighters, but that is ten Helot men for every one Spartan soldier.' As his words sank in, Lysander felt a mixture of dread and excitement. 'That is why every pure-born Spartan boy goes through the agoge. It is true that Helots fear us Spartans, but do not think that we are not afraid too. Our armies are useful for fighting conflicts in foreign lands, but their main purpose is to keep our own back gardens safe. Why do you think we declare the war each year? If the Helots wanted to, they could rise up at any time. They might not win, but there would be terrible bloodshed on both sides.' Lysander could hear something like fear in his grandfather's tone. 'The Helots are like a dry tinder – it needs only a spark to set rebellion alight.'

When the time came to say farewell, Lysander walked with Sarpedon to the road. His grandfather's words had shocked him. Every morning in the millhouse he had dreamt of a time when he could fight for Helot liberty. Was that day coming?

He offered his arm as usual, and was surprised when his grandfather took it and pulled him close in an embrace.

'Take care of yourself, my grandson, and I shall hope to see you soon.' They pulled apart and Sarpedon held Lysander by his shoulders.

'When will you be back?' Lysander asked.

'I cannot say, but it isn't likely to be before the full moon.'

'But that's the night of the Festival . . .' began Lysander. Sarpedon sighed.

'I would like to be there. But Sparta comes first. You have trained hard, and whether or not I am there in person, the spirit of Thorakis and your ancestors will be watching.'

Lysander nodded. He chose his words carefully.

'I hope you come back safely,' he said from his heart.

Sarpedon released him, and Lysander thought he saw the glistening of tears in his eyes.

'Goodbye, my grandson,' he said, turning away.

Lysander watched the Ephor leave. His brain was a confusion of loyalty and guilt. He had meant it when he wished his grandfather safety, but what he had *not* said was just as important. Of course he wished Sarpedon no harm, but he could not find it in his heart to hope for Spartan success. *What if this is a chance for the Helots to be free?*

As he made his way back to the barracks, he was blind to his surroundings. Images flashed through his mind. Argive soldiers marching through Spartan fields, cheered on by Helots. As he approached the barracks entrance, Lysander imagined the building, the symbol of Spartan might, ablaze, with red-cloaked soldiers fleeing a powerful Helot army.

'And where have you been sneaking out to, half-breed?' came a voice from the shadows of the doorway. Someone stepped out into the light. Demaratos.

'That's not your concern,' said Lysander, trying to squeeze past. Demaratos thrust his arm across the door-frame, and stepped close to Lysander, pushing him back against the wall.

'I know this is not the first time you have gone out.

I have heard you, tiptoeing out every morning. So I shall ask you again, what mischief is this?'

A noise behind Demaratos made Lysander peer over his enemy's shoulder. *What if it is Diokles?*

'I thought creeping around at night was something you Spartans were trained in,' he said to Demaratos.

'Oh, it is, Helot, but we are a lot better at it than you.'

Through a crack in the inner door to the equipment room, Lysander saw who was watching them – it was Prince Leonidas. His gently drooping eyes were fixed on them both. *Why did he not come to help?* Lysander didn't know what to do. He could not afford to get caught – it would mean a lashing from the barracks commander. He needed to be at his peak for the Festival. Still Leonidas's eyes were locked on his. Would Lysander's friend try to help him? Distract Demaratos or step out to break up the scene? Lysander waited.

'Shall I ring the alarm bell, Helot?' Demaratos was smiling now. 'Shall I wake up Diokles and see what he wants to do with you?'

Lysander was becoming angrier with Leonidas than with the boy in front of him. It was clear the prince was not going to help a Helot slave. Lysander pushed Demaratos's arm out of his way, and stormed into the equipment room.

'We will finish this later!' his tormentor called after him.

Inside the room, he saw Leonidas walking quickly

183

away past a pile of damaged shields. Lysander ran over to him and caught him by the shoulder, swinging him round. Leonidas looked shocked – and guilty.

'Lysander! What are you doing here?' Leonidas's false cheeriness fooled no one. Lysander and he both knew that the prince had been watching – and doing nothing.

'You're supposed to be my friend!' hissed Lysander. 'Why did you stand by and watch when Demaratos threatened me?'

A cloud passed over Leonidas's face. 'I . . . What are you talking about?' he said defensively.

But Lysander was not ready to let this go. He seized Leonidas by his collar and pulled him close. He wanted to throw the prince to floor, and call him a coward, the ultimate offence against a Spartan. But the inner door was pushed open, and four boys rushed into the room, laughing. They stopped when they saw Leonidas and Lysander squaring up to each other.

'What are you looking at?' said Lysander, his blood still hot. But his brain told him now was not the time to fight. He shoved Leonidas in the chest. The prince stumbled backwards.

Lysander watched the prince leave. He had learnt a new lesson today. Strength was no guarantee of bravery, and cowards were not always to be found among the enemy. They could be your friends, too.

CHAPTER 20

It did not take long for the news of the war against Argos to reach Sparta. Rumours spread through the dormitory like a river flooding its plain.

'They say forty Spartans faced a thousand men,' said Hilarion as they sat eating one evening. His father was away fighting, and his son got all the latest news. 'The Argives thought they would crush us, but the phalanx held firm. The enemy ended up trampling their own men to death, and many died with spears in their backs, running away.'

Prokles chipped in:

'Yes, and did you hear that the warrior Kleon challenged their best to single combat? He sliced his opponent's shield arm, but then spared him. A Spartan would never want to live without his left arm. He would rather die than be unable to join his comrades in the phalanx.'

But it was not all glory. There was news of death, also. As Lysander left the training yard one day to visit the latrine, he came across Hilarion sitting by the barracks wall in the shade. In his hands he clutched an adult helmet, and he was sobbing. Stepping closer, Lysander could see that the bronze crown of the helmet was marred by an ugly open gash – it looked as though a sword blow had torn through it. Lysander did not need to ask what had happened – Hilarion's father was dead.

As the conflict entered its second month, the stories died down. It began to look like the war was less than clear-cut. Some said the Athenians would help their neighbours and drive the Spartans away. Lysander lay awake at night thinking of the possible outcomes. Perhaps the soldiers of Argos were fighting back. Perhaps they would march into Spartan territory, driving the Spartans away to the sea. It would be a chance for Lysander's people to be free.

It was almost time for the late summer harvest. The fields were ripe again with barley, and the boys were out on a long march in full armour. They wore breast-plates, leg guards and helmets and carried their spears and shields. Lysander had hand-me-downs and unwanted kit from previous years. His breastplate and the apron that covered his groin were worn leather, frayed at the edges, and the bronze lining was flaking off. The greaves on his shins were rusted from not being properly cleaned, and his helmet was too tall and narrow for his head, blistering the tops of his ears and shaking loose every so often. On the night of the

Games they would have to present themselves to the spectators before the real competition began. Lysander dreaded to think what a sight he would make.

The midday sun pounded down, and all Lysander could see through the narrow slit of his helmet was the boy in front. The soles of his feet had become hard, and were ingrained with dust. Sweat glued his tunic to his body. He felt faint, and his tongue was thick and dry in his mouth. He longed for just a sip of cool water. They were rounding the turning point on their run, the shrine of Zeus, and heading back to camp, when the pounding of hooves pricked Lysander's ears. The others looked round as well.

'Halt!' Diokles held up an arm for the boys to stop, raising his spear.

Two horsemen burst from a copse of trees and galloped towards them. They were not Spartans. They carried light bows, with a quiver of arrows tied to the sides of their mounts. Small round shields were slung over their shoulders. Lysander felt dread fix him to the ground, but Diokles lowered his weapon and greeted the men with a salute.

'Megarans,' one of the boys whispered. 'You can tell from their shields. They are our allies against Argos.'

The two soldiers slowed to a canter as they approached the ranks of students, and Diokles stepped forward to take the reigns of the lead rider. The horse was small and lean, snorting and stamping its front foot. The horseman patted its neck until it was calm and dismounted. He was covered in dust.

'News from the plains of Argos,' said the Megaran, still panting. 'They sent us because we are the quickest . . .'

Lysander held his breath. Could the Argives be marching south, ready to free the Helot people?

'I come to announce a brilliant victory for Sparta,' continued the messenger. 'The Argives are completely vanquished.'

A cheer went up, but Lysander did not join in. The Helots' dreams were dashed.

'We must press on to the Council of Elders with the good news,' said the Megaran, swinging himself back on to his mount. 'Tell everyone you see that the glory of Sparta is intact.'

'Of course,' said Diokles. The two riders set off and soon crested the hill that led down to the Spartan valley beyond. Diokles turned to his students.

'It is a great day for Sparta. The enemy broke like waves upon our shields. As a celebration, there will be no more training today.'

The students raised another shout of joy. As they began the slow march back to camp, Lysander blocked the other boys' excited chatter from his mind. The Helots would never be free.

'Are you not happy, Helot?' It was Demaratos, and he was looking at Lysander in disgust. 'We have proven once again that Sparta is the most powerful city in all Greece.'

'Of course I am,' Lysander said, trying to mask his

anger. Demaratos was right. No one could conquer the Spartans.

Orpheus, Lysander and Leonidas sat at the back of the classroom while Anu demonstrated something he called an *abacus* from his native land. It was a wooden board threaded with beads for counting. Lysander was impressed with the way it could calculate sums quickly.

'Mathematics is boring,' grumbled Prokles. 'Counting is for free-dweller traders, not soldiers.'

'Is that right?' said Anu. 'And when you come to lead a campaign against your enemies, how will you calculate the amount of food your men need? I anticipate your glorious army would turn back before it even reached the battlefield, starving and humiliated.'

The Games were just two days away now, and few boys were interested in mathematics. Everyone was waiting for the squad leaders to announce their teams.

In the row in front of them, Demaratos was flexing his muscles, and talking about victory as though it were already his.

'My father says he will have a statue dedicated in my honour at the Temple of Ortheia,' he boasted. 'There is no boy in the barracks who can beat me. I've come first every year since I entered the agoge.'

Lysander bristled. He had been training hard and, despite still being without the Fire of Ares, he felt better than ever before. His new confidence gave him added strength. He came up alongside Demaratos.

189

'You should be careful, you know,' he said casually. 'The Gods do not favour proud mortals.'

Demaratos laughed.

'And who are you to talk to a Spartan about his Gods? I suppose you think you would be a match for me.' The rest of the class were watching, expecting a fight. Demaratos turned to his audience. 'Who here thinks Lysander can take me on? Who thinks a Helot could beat a Spartan?' The other boys looked away. Demaratos walked over and shoved Pausanias in the chest.

'Do you think Lysander would win, Pausanias?'

Pausanias shook his head. Demaratos pointed at Hilarion.

'What about you? Are you on the Helot's side?'

Hilarion was silent.

No one spoke up. Demaratos laughed cruelly at his easy victory, his eyes scanning the lowered heads around him. Only Lysander kept the bully's gaze. Demaratos shook his head.

'What a bunch of –'

Someone cleared his throat. Lysander looked round. It was Orpheus.

'I do!' said his friend.

Demaratos's smile slipped for a second – but only a second. Orpheus was well respected, but he was still only one boy.

'Anybody else?' Demaratos called out.

Come on, thought Lysander.

Demaratos was enjoying himself. 'I said, does anyone else think this snivelling Helot is a match for me?'

Lysander looked around, but all the other boys just stared at the ground.

'That is what I thought,' said Demaratos triumphantly. 'Just the Helot and the cripple. I have never seen two worse examples of Spartans.'

'I think he can beat you,' said a quiet voice. Lysander saw Leonidas step out from the back of the crowd. 'I'm going to put him on my team. Then we will really see who is best – in a *fair* fight.'

Lysander felt his throat tighten. After their argument, Lysander and Leonidas had been avoiding each other. He could imagine how difficult it must have been for Leonidas to take that small step forward. The prince had been born into a life of privilege, and Lysander had seen for himself that he struggled to always make the right choice. But for once, Leonidas had found strength of character. And for him – a Helot.

Demaratos looked astounded.

'If you want your team to lose, then go ahead,' he spat.

A few of the boys dared to lift their gazes from the ground and now they were watching Demaratos with open curiosity. They had probably never seen him challenged like this before, Lysander realised.

Demaratos fixed his eyes on Lysander.

'You think you are so tough, don't you, Helot? But I have a secret weapon, something that can really help me win . . .'

The Fire of Ares! It had to be.

'Don't let him trouble you,' muttered Orpheus, touching Lysander's arm. He shook it off.

A few other boys started to pay attention. *He's got it!* thought Lysander. *He's got the amulet. Is he wearing it now?* He stepped closer to Demaratos.

'And what might that be?' said Lysander, holding Demaratos's stare with his own. His enemy folded his arms and smiled knowingly at Lysander.

'Why, the heart of a Spartan warrior, of course.'

Demaratos marched out of the barracks.

'And the soul of a snake,' muttered Orpheus.

Lysander turned to Orpheus. Leonidas was standing with him.

'Thank you,' he said. He held a hand over Leonidas's shoulder and brought it down in a firm, friendly slap. Words were not necessary.

'We should get out there and train, if we are to beat that thug. I promised him a thrashing,' Leonidas said, nervously joking.

As they trooped across the yard, Lysander heard his name being called out. It was Diokles. He gestured from his quarters. Lysander ran over.

'Lysander, it is your mother . . .'

Lysander's skin went cold. 'Is she all right?'

'No. You are excused lessons for the afternoon to go and see her. Be back before sunset.'

Lysander ran all the way to the far side of Amikles, his

panic masking any tiredness in his legs. The only noise Lysander heard was the blood rushing in his ears.

With Sarpedon still away in the north, the villa seemed empty. Making his way across the mosaic tiles, Lysander was surprised to see Strabo. Normally an attendant would accompany his Spartan master to war. But then he remembered that Strabo was a freedweller. He was carrying a stack of linen.

'Greetings, Master Lysander,' he said.

'I was called to see my mother.'

'She's in her room. Kassandra has been looking after her.'

Lysander hurried to the chamber. He did not know what to expect. When he reached the curtain covering the door of the room, a noise made him hesitate. Someone was in there with Athenasia. He hooked a finger around the screen and peered inside.

Leaning over her patient with a damp cloth was Kassandra. She was wearing a simple cream tunic, tied in the middle with a black belt. Her black hair fell around her cheeks. Lysander's heart sank: his mother lay very still in the bed, her skin pale with blotches of red. The girl dabbed at her forehead. Lysander could see that her lips were moving, but he could not hear the comforting words she was offering. Was this really the same girl who had cursed him as a Helot not a few days before? He stepped into the room.

Kassandra looked up. Wordlessly, she passed him the cloth and walked out. The room smelled of citrus, no doubt from the medicines Athenasia had been given. There was another scent that Lysander did not recognise, coming from some blocks of yellow resin smoking on a low table. Tears of gratitude pricked at Lysander's eyes. The thought of his mother enduring her illness in their former hut was unbearable now.

He stepped to her side and took hold of her hand. The skin was dry and thin, stretched over the knuckle joints. Looking at her lying on the bed, Lysander thought that she seemed only half in this world. Her body was gradually giving up its spirit. He kissed the back of her hand. At the touch of his lips, her eyelids opened just a crack and she smiled. Lysander caught a glimpse of the old Athenasia, before the illness came upon her. A tear trickled down his cheek, and landed in the folds of his mother's blanket.

'What are you crying for, my boy?' she croaked.

'I cannot bear to see you like this,' he replied.

'Wrapped up in Spartan luxury?' she asked, smiling.

Lysander laughed shallowly through his tears.

'Are you in pain?' he asked.

'No, Lysander,' she said. 'I can feel very little. Kassandra – she has been good to me. A special girl.'

Lysander nodded his head and swallowed back more tears. He touched his mother's head with the cloth.

'Listen well, my son. I have lived a hard life, but not an unhappy one. Your father – Thorakis – he was a wonderful, brave, gentle man. I can see now that you

194

will be just like him – a Spartan warrior.' The tendons tightened under the skin of her neck as a silent coughing fit shook her body. She did not have the strength to fight it. Lysander held her thin shoulders. She gave a long sigh.

'Find the Fire of Ares, Lysander. Make me proud . . .'

'Please, Mother, not yet . . . do not leave me yet . . .'

'I will never leave you,' she said.

Athenasia's eyes closed.

Lysander's mother was dead.

By the time Lysander left the room, he was dry of tears. He had said his final farewell to his mother, and stroked her face until the warmth left it. He had never seen anyone die in front of him before. It was just like a candle going out.

Now the bright daylight stung the rims of his eyes, and the colours of the flowers in Sarpedon's garden came as a surprise to him. They seemed gaudy and irreverent. Soft steps behind him caught his attention. *Not Strabo again!* But it was Kassandra. She had lifted her hair away from her face, and tied it back with a long, ivory pin on top of her head.

'Is she . . .?'

Lysander nodded, fighting back fresh tears.

'Athenasia was a brave woman, and she loved you dearly,' said Kassandra.

His mother's name was like an open wound still, and Lysander could not help but lash out.

'Why would you care? She was just a Helot, like me . . .'

Kassandra flushed and let her eyes drop. Lysander immediately regretted his words.

'I'm sorry, I . . .' He stopped short as she put a hand on his shoulder.

'I misjudged you before,' she said quietly. 'We Spartans are taught that we are better than Helots, and it takes a lot to believe otherwise. I am not making excuses, but . . . well, your mother has made me realise I was wrong. I know you cannot forgive all of Sparta for enslaving your people, but maybe you can forgive me?'

Lysander was moved by her words.

'Thank you,' he said. 'Friends?'

'Yes, friends,' she smiled. 'Sarpedon is expected back this evening, and he will arrange for your mother's death-rites. You should get back to the barracks. I have heard Diokles is very strict.'

The name caught Lysander by surprise.

'But who has told you that?' he said. Kassandra's eyes dropped.

'Oh, no one . . .' Then, 'It must have been Sarpedon . . . or Strabo . . .' but her words were too quick.

Lies, thought Lysander.

'Who was the person I saw you talking to that day in the street?'

'Um . . . Oh, you mean the other morning? He was a tradesman. I was arranging supplies for my horse.' She sounded sure of herself, and Lysander felt guilty for supposing she was up to something. He started to leave, but she called him back.

'Lysander, tell me one thing. When your mother first came here, she mumbled something in her fever about a Fire of Ares. She said you had to find it. What did she mean?'

Lysander paused in his tracks. Could he trust her? He was not sure. They were cousins, part of the same family, but until today she had shown him nothing but contempt. On the other hand, his mother had said she was a good person. He decided to tell her the bare minimum.

'It is an amulet,' he said. 'A red stone that belonged to my father. It's very special to me.'

'It sounds beautiful,' she said. 'I truly hope you find it.'

Lysander was touched by her concern. His emotions were in tatters.

'Well, goodbye,' he said, 'and thank you for the care you gave to my mother.'

'Goodbye, Lysander,' she replied.

As Lysander started back towards the barracks, thoughts of the Fire of Ares soon fell from his mind. He would never sit and eat a meal with his mother again, never hear her laugh or see her smile. His heart was heavy with grief. But there was also hope. And determination. His parents were both dead now, but he would make them proud.

CHAPTER 21

The night of the Festival Games had arrived.

Lysander was buckling on his battered breastplate. Though Timeon had done his best with the polishing, there was no hiding that his equipment was second-hand, left by a boy in the year above him. It was small, too, and pinched his chest in the tight straps. Demaratos's armour gleamed like the sun. Every boy wore a new red cloak to symbolise passing to the next level. All but Lysander. He still made do with the tattered reminder of Athandros.

'You bring shame to the barracks,' Demaratos scoffed. A few boys turned, but most were focused on preparing themselves for the parade.

'Your clothes are of no importance,' replied Lysander. 'It is how you behave that counts.'

'Well, you had better be on your best behaviour,' said Prokles.

A creak came from the doorway at the far end of the barracks. Timeon ran in, carrying a bundle wrapped in sackcloth. He placed it on the bed carefully.

'What have you got there?' asked Lysander.

It took his friend some time to regain his breath.

'Why don't you have a look?' he said.

Lysander leant down and folded back the material. He gasped. There was a stiffened leather breastplate, covered in a layer of bronze, with a lion's head drawn in fine silver lines. That was not all: there were two matching leg guards and arm fastenings, each showing the design of a lion's claw. A helmet with a red crest completed the set. The workmanship was breathtaking. There was also a sheathed sword and silver-studded belt. *I can't believe it,* he thought. Looking up, he saw that Timeon was beaming from ear to ear.

'They are from Sarpedon,' he said. 'Strabo brought them here for you. They belonged to both his sons when they each passed through the agoge.'

'My grandfather is back?' said Lysander, testing the weight of the sword. He could see his reflection in the polished surface.

'Yes,' said Timeon. 'Strabo said the two Ephors and the king arrived back yesterday on horseback. The soldiers are marching a day behind.'

With Timeon's help, Lysander clipped on the armour. It fitted perfectly. He knew what this meant – it was more than a gift. Sarpedon was telling everyone that Lysander was his grandson. There would be no more secrets. Ariston and Prokles stared.

'That is the mark of Thorakis, from the house of

Sarpedon,' Prokles said, gazing round at his friends in astonishment. 'Lysander must be . . .'

He did not have a chance to finish what he was saying. Demaratos pushed through the crowd, shoving the boy aside.

'It will take more than fancy craftsmanship to give you victory tonight, half-breed.'

'Well,' said Lysander, 'may the best Spartan win.' He offered his hand to Demaratos, who slapped it away and left the dormitory. An uncertain ripple of laughter escaped the other Spartan students.

'I would ignore him,' said Orpheus at his side. Lysander wondered what this night would be like for the lame Spartan: he wouldn't be taking part in the ceremony or the Games because of his bad leg. But Orpheus surprised him.

'Here,' he said to Lysander, holding out his own new cloak, 'take this.' It took Lysander a moment to understand. A Spartan's cloak was his symbol of power, his second skin. For Orpheus to make a gift of his touched Lysander to the core.

'I cannot –'

'Don't be foolish,' Orpheus cut in. 'You can't wear that ragged thing with your new armour. Please, take it, I would be honoured. Just make sure you win.'

The ranks of boys made their approach to the Temple of Ortheia for the start of the Festival. It was a cloudless night, and the light from the moon and stars twinkled on the polished shields. As they drew near the temple, the way was lit on either side by flaming torches and the smell of incense drifted on a light breeze.

Tonight, Lysander was proud to be a Spartan, and prouder still to be representing the squad of Prince Leonidas.

Spectators lined the shallow grassy banks on three sides of the parade ground. Most were Spartans, mothers and fathers of the students, but there were also a few wealthy free-dwellers. Helot slaves rushed around, purchasing snacks and drinks for their masters. At the fourth side stood the temple. Lysander had only ever seen the structure before from a distance, when its red columns gleamed in the sun: six across the front, and thirteen along the side. Now, as it rose beside them it was by far the most spectacular building Lysander had ever seen. Above the columns scenes of hunting were carved into the stone: an archer stood ready to fire on a stag, while dogs reared around his feet. Lysander longed to know what was inside the temple. But he knew he would never be allowed to enter. Only priests and other initiates were permitted to witness the mysteries of the Goddess Artemis Ortheia.

There was a clash of cymbals and Diokles called them to stop. The crowd fell silent and turned their heads towards the temple.

Five young women, dressed in gleaming white tunics, emerged from between the two central columns of the temple entrance. To Lysander, they seemed to glide down the steps. Three held a single wreath of olive leaves, and one held a deep drinking bowl in both hands. The fifth held a kithara – a sacred lyre. Once they had taken position either side of the altar, she began to pluck its strings. The notes rang clear in the still air, and the music seemed to cast a spell over the spectators. The other four girls began to sing. The words were holy, a prayer to the Goddess Artemis Ortheia:

> *Hear us, Guardian of this sanctuary and of Sparta herself.*
> *Hear us, Artemis Ortheia.*
> *We honour the Gods always, and this night we honour you*
>   *above all.*
> *Bless these young men.*
> *They offer themselves to the Goddess in the name of*
>   *Sparta.*
> *Bless their spears, bless their shields and bless their blood*
> *We pray they will one day give all three to you in battle.*

As their song drew to a close, a tall robed man stepped out from the temple with two bare-chested attendants – young Spartan soldiers in their prime. The priest's face was enclosed in a terracotta mask – a symbol that he was sacred to Ortheia. As he approached, the priest-esses drifted soundlessly out of the way, until he alone stood in front of the altar. Holding up his arms, he intoned:

'In the name of the Ortheia, Great Huntress and

Protector of the Young, bring out the sacrifice.'

From behind the temple came a soft lowing, as the great bulk of a white ox was led out by a rope. It surveyed the crowds with heavy, doleful eyes. Its horns had been painted gold and red markings were drawn over its flanks. *It must not know it's about to be killed*, thought Lysander. The bull stood calmly as the priest took out a long knife, sparkling with precious stones, and placed it against the animal's throat.

'Mighty Ortheia, we offer to you this creature from our fields, that you will bless this night of celebration.'

The holy man stroked the beast's head as the two Spartans positioned themselves on either side. The priest slid the knife quickly into the animal's throat. The creature spasmed, but was steadied by the Spartan helpers. Lysander saw the priest twist his wrist and withdraw the blade. As the point cleared the dewlap, a fountain of blood spurted on to the ground, splashing the priest's feet. The bull's front knees buckled, and it sank to the ground, lolling on to its flank. As its eyes rolled back, the flow of blood pumping from the gash became less. The female attendant came forward with the bowl and filled it with the thick liquid. Lysander could not help but think of Cato, slaughtered in cold blood like an animal.

Remember where you come from, he told himself. *Make the Helots proud.*

When he looked up again, the bull was lying on its side, its chest heaving slowly as it lay in the dust. The priestess knelt beside it, gathering blood in a shallow bowl. Later, the meat would be eaten in celebration, the bones and entrails burned as an offering to the Gods.

Now came the dance. The boys lined up in front of the crowd of spectators, each holding a shield and spear. Lysander could not see Sarpedon among the sea of faces, though he knew he must be there somewhere.

A clash of cymbals heralded the start of the sequence, and drums kept them in time. Lysander and the others stepped, lunged and parried imaginary attacks, all in unison. Lysander knew his part off by heart. He didn't need to look to his side, and anyway, the narrow slits in his helmet prevented him from seeing much more than the boy in front. By the end, he was sweating, but proud. The audience cheered the display.

After the dancing ended, the two teams separated from the other boys to begin the wrestling contest.

A pit of about twenty feet square had been filled with sand, which was now being raked over. Lysander stood on one side, his back to the ring, preparing himself by rubbing oil on his torso and legs. It would help him escape the clinches of his opponent. Lysander had been drawn against Sinon, a fast and devious member of Demaratos's team. But he was confident. He had seen Sinon fighting in the barracks, and he thought he could beat him even without the Fire of

Ares. But Timeon had bad news.

'Sinon had to drop out of Demaratos's team unexpectedly,' his friend told him, as he rubbed oil into Lysander's back. 'So, it's a replacement.'

Lysander didn't like the tone of Timeon's voice. He turned round.

'What is it, Timeon? What are you not telling me?'

'Well . . . erm . . . the replacement is quite, well . . . big.' Timeon looked unsure and he wiped his hands on a cloth.

'How big is big?' asked Lysander, feeling worried.

'That big,' said Timeon, pointing over his shoulder. Lysander swivelled round and saw a figure standing a head above the rest of Demaratos's team.

Drako!

He must have recovered from the flogging! He had not been in the parade. Lysander felt as though all his blood had turned to water and was trickling away.

'Do not panic,' said Timeon. 'You know what they say: The bigger the tree, the louder the crash when it falls in the forest.'

'I know,' said Lysander, squaring his shoulders, and trying to sound hopeful. 'I only hope I am not underneath the tree when it does.'

Timeon smiled unsurely and gave him a hard pat on the back.

'Good luck, Lysander.'

He stepped into the ring. Drako eyed him from across the sand. The crowd cheered raucously.

'Hello, Lysander,' he said. 'It is time to suffer for what you did to me.'

'What do you mean?' Lysander asked. But the referee stepped between them. He was a young man dressed in a short white toga trimmed with Spartan red. He carried a thin, flexible rod made of elm wood, which he now held out between the two boys.

'You both know the rules, I am sure. The winner is the best of three points. A point is scored when your opponent's back is held to the floor, when they step outside the ring, or when they declare submission.'

Lysander looked around for a final time, trying to spot Sarpedon in the crowd, but if he was watching he was not making himself known.

The referee continued: 'There is to be no kicking to the groin, no gouging of the eyes, and no biting. Other than that, anything goes. Honour the Gods and be brave.'

He lifted the rod and the crowd came alive, shouting encouragement for both sides. The fight was on. He heard Timeon's voice: 'You can do it, Lysander!' But he also heard Demaratos's voice: 'Crush him, Drako. Make him wish he had stayed in the fields.'

Lysander swallowed, and looked at the giant in front of him. Lysander could see the criss-crossed scarring over his shoulders and bulging arms. Drako grinned back, showing his line of missing teeth.

The two boys circled one another. Lysander looked at his opponent's massive upper body. *I have to get close,*

206

he thought. *No use staying at range, where he has the advantage.* He threw himself forward, landing an elbow under Drako's ribs. The giant did not budge, and turned Lysander, gripping him around the lower part of his chest. Lysander was trapped with his back to his opponent.

'Is that all your strength, Helot?' he whispered, tightening his grip. 'Demaratos told me what you did,' he said into Lysander's ear. 'It was you who informed on me to Diokles.' Lysander tried to answer, but he could not. The air was being squeezed out of him as he was lifted off the floor. His arms were pinioned, his legs dangling uselessly.

He bent his neck forward and then threw his head backwards into the other boy's face. Drako let out a howl as Lysander's skull crunched into his nose. The pain forced him to loosen his grip. As soon as Lysander felt the ground beneath his feet, he seized hold of Drako's ankle, and pulled it sharply upwards between his own legs. Like a toppling pine, Drako had no choice but to fall to the ground. Lysander flattened himself against the giant, pinning him to the sand.

'One point to Lysander,' shouted the referee. A cheer erupted from Lysander's supporters. Red-faced, Drako threw him off as though he weighed nothing more than a heavy blanket.

'You were lucky,' he muttered through a grimace.

'Listen, Drako, I had nothing to do with Diokles. Demaratos is lying!'

'Round two!' said the referee, lifting his rod.

This time Lysander went straight for the legs, hooking his arms around both of Drako's knees. But he could not knock the bigger boy over – he was like a boulder. Drako unhooked himself, and twisted Lysander's arm behind his back, kneeling over him. Then he began to apply pressure upwards, and pain shot through Lysander's wrist, elbow and shoulder. He started to feel his tendons stretch, and did the only thing he could.

'Submission!' he yelled, tapping Drako's leg with his free hand. He hated giving up, but it was better than a broken arm. With a final twist, Drako released him.

'One apiece,' said the referee, as both boys regained their feet. 'Final round!'

As Lysander climbed to his feet, he heard a familiar voice.

'You can do it, Lysander!'

He looked up to see Leonidas standing beside Timeon. Lysander nodded his head in thanks.

'Come on!' shouted Timeon, pumping a fist.

A few other voices in the crowd cheered their support, but Demaratos shouted over them.

'Tear off his arms, Drako.'

'Remember the whip,' Ariston added. 'Remember what he did to you.'

Lysander faced Drako once more. They circled each other tentatively.

The rumblings from the spectators increased in

volume. Lysander could no longer hear Demaratos and his gang over their shouts. Gradually, more and more people joined in until he realised they were all behind him. *Come on, Lysander! You can do it!* They clapped their hands and stamped their feet in encouragement.

But this time he had to be more careful. He could not take Drako on in a straight fight. He had to be clever, and hit him on the counter-attack, or use the bigger boy's strength against him. So, when the first few lunges came in, Lysander ducked out of the way, or slipped Drako's grasp. Every time he did so, the spectators gasped. His opponent began to lumber slightly in the sand. *He is becoming tired!* thought Lysander. Now he was ready to spring his own attack. Checking the edge of the ring was close, he bent his knees and feinted an attack. Drako saw his chance and came forward a few steps, swinging an arm wildly. *Got him!* Lysander grabbed his opponent's outstretched arm, and pulled him forward. At the same time he twisted his body away and levered Drako off the ground. With a final tug, Lysander hurled the massive boy over his hip. He landed in a spray of sand, and was about to get up, when the referee's rod was shown to his face. Drako's rage turned to confusion, as the referee pointed to where his foot was lying: just outside the ring. It was over.

'Lysander wins!' cried the referee.

CHAPTER 22

'How are you feeling,' asked Timeon, as he helped scrape the sand away.

'Better than expected,' replied Lysander. His left arm was sore where it had been twisted up behind his back. Thankfully, he would not need it for the second event, the javelin, or the final foot race, if he got that far.

'Leonidas won his wrestling bout, too,' Timeon told him. 'So did three others from your team. Five of Demaratos's team went through.'

Demaratos threw first, crossing his legs in three long steps and then releasing his javelin. The crowd drew a collective breath and the javelin left his hand at a perfect angle. The shaft did not even wobble as it cut through the air, and then dropped into the ground: *Phut!*

Lysander was tense as he made his way forward to throw the javelin. Would he make it through this round? His skills had improved a good deal since that first lesson, and though his arm was strong through all his extra training with Sarpedon, his technique still needed work. But Leonidas and Demaratos were the strongest throwers, for sure.

Lysander pushed his fingers into the leather thong, and stretched his arm. He recited Diokles' advice in his mind: *Don't look at the spear, look at where you are throwing it.* He looked into the night sky, and saw the pattern of stars known as the Twins — Kastor and Polydeukes.

He took his steps and released the javelin. Though the shaft gave a little shudder, it settled in smooth flight. It landed in fifth spot so far, behind Demaratos and three other members of his team: Ariston, Prokles and Meleager. But Leonidas was still to throw. This meant Lysander would not go through to the foot race. He was disappointed, but he had tried his best.

The prince was nowhere to be seen. He looked over to where the others were all warming up. Demaratos and Prokles looked relaxed, chatting to each other with smiles on their faces. One of them cast a glance to a boy at the side of the stadium, clutching his middle. He looked up. It was Leonidas! Lysander hurried over to his friend.

'What is wrong?' he asked.

The prince's face was pale and covered with a sheen of sweat. He looked like a corpse.

'I feel awful,' said Leonidas. 'My stomach keeps cramping. I got through the wrestling, but I don't think I can throw the javelin.'

'But you have to,' said Lysander. 'It must be nerves. Here, let me help you.' He took Leonidas's arm over his shoulder and lifted his friend to his feet. The prince walked gingerly forward and was handed a javelin by a Helot. He looked about to collapse at any moment. On unsteady legs, he launched the javelin. The crowd let out a groan. It was a terrible throw, landing well short of the others.

Leonidas was out of the competition.

And that meant Lysander was still in.

The prince did not walk far again before pitching forward. He vomited on to the ground. Lysander rushed towards him and rubbed Leonidas's back while he waited for him to finish retching.

Lysander heard laughter and turned to see Ariston talking with Demaratos and Prokles.

'Maybe that second helping of stew did not sit well,' suggested Ariston innocently.

Of course! Lysander remembered now. Ariston's Helot, Chrysippus, had served them a second helping. Lysander had given his to Timeon, who had said he didn't like the taste. He should have known; Timeon never passed up a meal.

'He's poisoned you!' he said to Leonidas. *I'll show him* . . . He began to walk off, but Leonidas made a grab for his leg.

'Don't!' he scolded. 'It won't help to get into a fight now.'

'But what are we going to do?' asked Lysander. 'I'm

not as fast as you. I can't win the foot race!

Leonidas smiled.

'Have faith. You've not won the foot race before. That doesn't mean you *can't* win it. Don't tire yourself out on the first leg and then give it everything on the home straight.'

There was something about the tone of Leonidas's voice that gave Lysander a shred of hope. He was now the only representative from the prince's team. Leonidas had shown faith in him, and he would do his best to repay that.

Two parallel ropes were stretched across the start line, one at knee level and one at the waist. When these were released on a spring mechanism, the race would begin. The starting line was marked by a sunken stone block, into which was cut a long groove to push off from. Lysander pressed the ball of his foot against this gutter, and looked to his left and right. Now that Leonidas had been forced to drop out, only five boys were lined up. Immediately to his left was Prokles, and to his right was Ariston, Meleager and finally Demaratos.

The air was still. Two lengths of the stadium, that was all. Lysander focused on the turning post facing him at the far end and remembered Leonidas's advice. *Don't tire yourself out on the first leg.* The referee holding the starting post called them to make themselves ready. Lysander poised himself to spring forward.

The ropes jumped to the floor and the crowd let out a cheer. The race was on.

Demaratos left the block like a charging wild boar. Lysander was slower to get going, but soon found a rhythm. Most of the boys were a few paces ahead of him after his poor start. The Spartans in the crowd were cheering Demaratos, and Lysander kept glimpsing his rival through the bodies. He could feel Prokles right on his shoulder, but focused all his attention on the turning post ahead. By the time he reached it, he was not tired, and he was almost level with Ariston and Meleager. He rounded the post, digging the hardened soles of his feet into the ground for extra grip. Just as he was ready to set off on the return leg, he felt someone snatch at his arm. Prokles! His leg slipped and he fell to his hands and knees. By the time he had righted himself and pulled away, the rest of the field were streaking ahead.

At the far end of the stadium, Timeon stood waving his arms, his mouth moving in wild shouts. Lysander could not hear what he was saying, because of the screams of the Spartans in the crowd. By halfway along the stadium, he was beginning to close in on Meleager and Ariston. But his legs burned and his lungs did not seem big enough.

The shouts for Demaratos had vanished now and another name was being chanted. It took him a second to realise what it was: 'LY-SAN-DER, LY-SAN-DER, LY-SAN-DER!' Helots and Spartans alike were cheering his name.

He eased past Meleager.

Now he could focus on Demaratos for the first time, pounding to his right, his breath misting in the night air.

Come on! Lysander told himself.

Ariston tripped near the edge of the stadium, and sprawled into the ground face first.

The crowd gasped.

Just Demaratos to catch.

Lysander's leg muscles were like rods of fire. He imagined that the air he sucked in was water putting out the flames.

Nearly there!

Timeon's mouth was wide with shouts that Lysander could not hear. He did not even have the energy to look and see where Demaratos was.

With a final push Lysander dived for Timeon on the line.

He untangled himself from his friend. Lysander looked across to see Demaratos whooping for joy – he had his arms in the air and his friends were gathered around celebrating. Lysander's heart sank. *I lost. I let Demaratos beat me!* He tried to tell Timeon about Prokles, but the words came out confused.

'He . . . Prokles . . .' he pointed. 'I couldn't . . . cheated . . .'

But as they watched, the starting referee walked over

to Demaratos's group, followed by two cloaked attendants. They spoke hurriedly, the referee motioning with his rod at Prokles. Then they all looked in Lysander's direction. Demaratos tried to say something, looking furious, but the referee shook his head. Prokles looked afraid. Next thing, the two attendants took hold of an arm each and began to pull him away. Timeon ran over to investigate.

When Lysander's friend skidded back to his side, he had some interesting news.

'The referee said the race was not run fairly. Prokles has been taken away to be flogged for offending the Gods.'

'But Demaratos has still won −'

'No,' interrupted Timeon. 'The referee says it is a tie. There will be a decider!'

The adrenalin had long stopped flowing and Lysander lay back exhausted. Timeon sat on the ground beside him, holding out a flask of water. Lysander took long, slow swallows.

'I'm not sure I can keep going,' he said.

'You will when I tell you what I have discovered,' replied Timeon. He leant closer to Lysander's ear. 'I know who took the Fire of Ares!'

CHAPTER 23

'Who?' Lysander asked.

Timeon nodded his head in the direction of a Helot filling up a water jug. He had his back to them, but when he stood and turned, Lysander recognised him straight away. It was Demaratos's slave.

'Boas stole the Fire of Ares?' said Lysander in disbelief. They watched as the Helot limped cautiously over to his master with the water. Demaratos snatched the flask, and pushed Boas angrily away.

'He didn't want to, but he was obeying Demaratos's orders. At that time, neither of them knew that you were more than a common Helot.'

Lysander stood up.

'I will kill that thief!'

But Timeon held him back.

'Lysander, stop. Demaratos hasn't got the pendant.'

'I don't care if he hasn't got it *now*,' retorted Lysander, struggling to pull away from Timeon's grip. 'It must be back at the barracks. I'll show him . . .'

'No, Lysander, you do not understand,' said Timeon. 'Demaratos didn't want the Fire of Ares for himself. He wanted it for his girlfriend. As a gift.'

Lysander stopped fighting, and looked at his friend. 'His girlfriend? Where would someone like Demaratos find a –'

'Over there,' interrupted Timeon, pointing into the crowd. Lysander followed his finger.

It couldn't be! Timeon was pointing straight at the girl standing beside a cloaked Spartan. He realised the Spartan was Sarpedon. Beside him, wearing a fine dress of indigo fabric, stood Kassandra.

Two Helots dragged rakes across the sand, turning over the patches where blood had dripped from the wounds of previous contestants. Lysander was beyond worrying about cuts and bruises. He was angrier than ever. *Kassandra and Demaratos!* Now it all made sense. Demaratos was the Spartan he had seen outside the Ephor's house the morning of his argument with Kassandra. The love token in the barracks was from her. Demaratos must have known all along that he was the grandson of Sarpedon. Timeon had started to reapply oil from the flask.

'How did you find all this out?' he asked his friend.

'Boas told me himself. I found him after the wrestling. When you beat Drako he hurled a jar at Boas's foot, and broke two of his toes. That is why he's limping. Well, for Boas, that was enough. He can be talkative when he is upset. He told me all about the mistreatment Demaratos doles out to him – the beatings, the name-calling. He is tired of it – he wants revenge. So he told me about the morning at the market. After you fought with Demaratos in the alleyway, he was told to find where you lived back at the Helot settlement. He went to the physician, who told him. After that, it was just a matter of following you among the stalls the next day, and stealing the amulet.'

It all fits into place! thought Lysander.

'I was being watched that morning by the millhouse,' he said to Timeon, 'but by a Helot – Boas!'

More than anything, Lysander wondered about Kassandra. So it was Boas she was meeting that morning outside Sarpedon's villa. No doubt she was handing over a token of her love for Demaratos. The depth of her treachery made him sick.

'I wonder if she's wearing it now,' he said bitterly. 'She knows it was stolen from me! She must do.'

He looked at her face, smiling back at him.

How could she? After looking after my mother?

One thing was for certain: they could never be friends again.

The time had come. The cymbals clashed. Timeon slapped him on the shoulder.

'May the Gods bless you,' he said.

Lysander faced Demaratos. His torso glistened in the

light from the stars, and his eyes were nothing but black holes in his face. This would settle things once and for all. The crowd was silent as the referee stepped between them.

'You both know the rules for the tie-break. The best of five points.'

It began.

Demaratos and Lysander were roughly the same height and weight. They circled each other. Lysander watched his opponent's arms and legs. Demaratos moved like a cat, light on its feet, stalking its prey.

'Are you scared, Helot?' taunted the Spartan. 'When I have finished with you, you will wish you were picking weeds in the fields. Like your friend . . . Cato.'

The name of the murdered Helot came as a surprise to Lysander, and Demaratos must have seen his concentration slip. Demaratos lunged forward, trying to wrap his arms around Lysander's neck. Lysander blocked the attack on the inside with both forearms. The two boys stood, face to face, each grasping the other's shoulders.

'How do you know about Cato?' Lysander demanded.

Demaratos spat back. 'You would go the same way, if I had my choice.'

Lysander struggled to force Demaratos's head down, but his opponent locked his legs.

'You're a common thief,' said Lysander.

Demaratos laughed.

'So, you know about that? Not so tough without

your necklace, are you?' grinned Demaratos. 'I hear you didn't show much courage that day either . . .'

Lysander felt his strength fading, and he was losing his grip on Demaratos's shoulder. He let go slightly to gain a better hold, but it was a mistake. As soon as his arm was freed, Demaratos let his own arm fold and swung his elbow into Lysander's nose. There was a crunch and he fell to the ground in a heap. His eyes streamed, and the tears mixed with something on his chin: blood.

'One point to Demaratos,' came the referee's cry, and a cheer went up from the crowd. 'Are you all right to go on?' Lysander held a hand gingerly to his face. His nose was tender and swollen. He found that he could move the bridge between his forefinger and thumb: definitely broken.

'I'm fine,' he said, wiping the blood from his face, and standing up. He saw Timeon's face etched with anxiety on the edge of the ring, but turned away.

This time Demaratos was confident: he looked powerful, larger than life. He came straight for Lysander with a ferocious kick, which he just managed to dodge. Demaratos did not stop coming forward. A left fist caught Lysander on the ear, sending him sprawling to the floor. Demaratos was on top of him, arm locked around his throat, and Lysander could not breathe. As the air left his lungs, doubts flooded his heart. *If only I had the Fire of Ares . . .*

But then he saw Sarpedon's face in the crowd. He

was looking straight at Lysander, and as he did, a voice entered his head: *You don't need the Fire of Ares. Your strength is in your blood: your Spartan blood and your Helot blood combined. Prove yourself today, son of Thorakis and Athenasia.*

Power flooded his sinews. With a mighty heave, he shrugged Demaratos away, then turned and punched with both hands to his opponent's chest. Demaratos stumbled backwards, his eyes wide with shock. Lysander did not give him a chance to regain his balance. He swept Demaratos off his feet, then knelt astride his chest, pinning his arms to the floor. Demaratos twisted and turned beneath him, but there was no way to escape. The referee took one look and held up his rod. One point each.

As Lysander was moving off Demaratos, he whispered in his ear.

'You should not have involved Kassandra. The Fire of Ares is stolen property.'

Demaratos stiffened beneath him, and Lysander took his position on the side of the ring. The crowd was shouting now. There was a new look on Demaratos's face: fear. He was slow to pick himself up. The tables had turned.

Lysander felt invincible as they squared off for the third round. As the referee lifted his rod, Lysander advanced. Demaratos's hand shot up, and suddenly Lysander could not see. He was blinded. It took him a few moments to realise what was in his eyes. *Sand!*

As he struggled to blink away the grit, Demaratos launched a savage attack. Blows fell on his head and ribs. Lysander kept his elbows into his body and shielded his face with his hands. *You fool*, he cursed, *you forgot what Sarpedon told you: a man is most dangerous when he's nearest to defeat.* He grabbed one of Demaratos's wrists, then the other. As his opponent struggled to free himself, Lysander let himself fall backwards. Demaratos had no choice but to follow. Lysander raised his foot against Demaratos's chest, not in a kick, but as a pivot. As his own back hit the ground he heard Demaratos shout. Lysander threw Demaratos's body over his head with his outstretched foot. He could not see, but he could imagine Demaratos somersaulting headlong through the air.

Lysander climbed to his feet and rubbed frantically at his eyes. He was expecting Demaratos to leap back at him, fired for revenge. It did not happen. He realised Timeon was talking to him.

'Move your hands, Lysander – I have water.'

Lysander did as he was told, and cold water splashed in his face. His vision cleared. Timeon stood in front of him, bucket in hand. The crowd was quiet, and Demaratos was at the edge of the ring, cradling his upper arm, his chest heaving. Lysander started to walk over, to finish Demaratos off, but the referee stepped between them.

'It's over,' he commanded.

'No!' shouted Demaratos. 'I can still fight.'

But Lysander saw the swelling around Demaratos's shoulder. There was a lump where the head of his humerus bone had been dislocated.

'The fight is over!' said the referee.

'Let me go on,' pleaded Demaratos.

The referee pushed lightly with his rod on the misshapen injury. Demaratos yelled as his face contorted in agony. There was clearly no way he could continue. He looked utterly deflated.

Demaratos had cheated, and he had lost.

The spectators began clapping, and murmuring their approval, growing louder until their cheers reached a crescendo. Lysander held his arm aloft to acknowledge them.

But why do I feel so empty? he asked himself. These people were clapping for him, were they not? Was this not the acceptance he'd always craved: to be recognised as a warrior, a winner? He looked again at the flushed faces of the crowd, their mouths twisted with the violence and the brutality. *Yes, I am a Spartan*, thought Lysander, *but at what cost?*

Lysander knelt before the altar of Ortheia, where the ground was still stained by the blood of the sacrifice. As the priest spoke a few words in honour of the Gods, one of the priestesses brought forth an olive wreath and handed it to the holy man. Lysander knew the prize was symbolic only. His name would be noted in the sanctuary, so everyone would know that Lysander, son of Thorakis, had triumphed at the Festival Games. After the priest had placed the wreath on his head, Lysander stood up, and the crowd cheered once again. In that moment, surrounded by strangers, he wished that his mother could have been there to witness his triumph. He was sure no one could see the tears that misted his eyes.

A trainer had appeared by the ring, and was inspecting Demaratos's swollen shoulder. At his instructions Demaratos lay on his side, as a physician took hold of his upper arm. Even in the torchlight, Demaratos looked pale and worried. With a heave, the trainer pulled the arm back into its socket. Demaratos let out a whimper, but nothing more. Tentatively he lifted his elbow – the joint was reset. Lysander spotted Kassandra – she was standing behind the trainer and now moved forward, placing a hand on Demaratos's arm. The sight made Lysander's anger flare up once again, and he couldn't help himself. He stormed over towards Kassandra. Demaratos tried to step between them, but Lysander pushed him aside.

'May the Gods curse you, Kassandra,' he snapped.

A look of puzzlement passed over her face.

'No, Lysander,' said Demaratos. Lysander ignored him.

'You haven't a drop of kindness in you, have you, *cousin*?'

'What do you mean?' asked Kassandra, backing away.

Lysander took hold of her wrist. 'Are you wearing it

now?' he said. He wanted to hear her admit to being a traitor.

'Wearing what?' she said, her eyes widening as Lysander tightened his grip.

'You dare to deny that you had the Fire of Ares all this time?' he said.

'The Fire of . . . ? I don't have it. I don't know what you're speaking of –'

'It's true,' interrupted Demaratos. 'She hasn't got the pendant. I never gave it to her.'

Now Lysander felt confusion wash through him. He let go of Kassandra's arm and faced Demaratos. His enemy dropped his head in shame, then cast a furtive glance at Kassandra.

'I took it for you, Kassandra. I wanted you to have it. It was a jewel worthy of a princess, too good for a Helot.'

'Then give it back now,' said Lysander coldly. He was ready to tear Demaratos to pieces.

'I no longer have it,' said Demaratos.

'Then who has?' Lysander demanded.

A shadow passed behind him. He realised someone was right there.

'It seems Demaratos cannot keep a secret,' said a growling voice.

Lysander whipped around to find Diokles standing far too close for comfort. The tutor pulled aside his tunic. Around his neck, scarlet in the moonlight, hung the Fire of Ares.

226

CHAPTER 24

'Come with me . . .' said Diokles, clamping Lysander's arm with his hand. 'I need your help in the equipment room.' The feasting had begun, and tables were being erected around the parade ground. Musicians were playing, and acrobats had begun their dancing.

Lysander found himself dragged behind the temple to the long building where they had taken off their armour after the demonstration. A few boys still lingered there, but Diokles threw them out.

When they were alone, Diokles closed the door behind him. The room was lit by candles along each wall, and the flickering lights played across Diokles' face, making his expression shift ghoulishly.

'You fought well tonight, Lysander,' he said, without smiling. 'Who would have thought a Helot like you would come out top at the Festival?'

'That pendant belongs to me,' Lysander said.

Diokles' hand caressed the stone, and he laughed as he brushed it with his fingers.

'You know very well, Lysander, that a Helot owns no property of his own.'

'And you know very well,' said Lysander, 'that I am not a Helot . . .'

'Ha!' scoffed Diokles. 'You think, because you have spent a summer training in the agoge, that you are one of us? It will take more than a lucky victory to call yourself a Spartan. Demaratos is still twice the warrior you will ever be.'

Lysander flinched, but wouldn't back down.

'When I have mastered the Spartan arts of lying, cheating and stealing, maybe then I will be his equal.'

Diokles laughed again.

'Yes, but even Demaratos needs to learn when to keep his mouth shut. I caught him bragging to those friends of his about a stolen jewel.' As he spoke, he lifted the strap from around his neck and took a step closer to Lysander. After so long, Lysander could not take his eyes off the stone, which glowed brighter than ever in the tutor's grimy hand. Lysander felt its presence like it was a part of him.

'At first,' said Diokles, 'I thought it was nothing, but when I laid my eyes upon it, I knew immediately it was no ordinary stone – the Fire of Ares!'

'How do you know so much about it?' Lysander asked.

Diokles ignored him and turned the pendant over, staring at the markings on the back.

'You will not know what this says?' he said.

Lysander remembered his mother's words: he knew exactly what the pendant said.

'Well, I'll tell you. It says *The Fire of Ares shall inflame the righteous.*'

'I know that,' said Lysander. 'It belonged to Menelaos, at the time of the war with Troy.'

'Very good,' said Diokles, raising his eyebrows in surprise. 'That's one part of its story. But, like men, stories change. We have been looking for the Fire of Ares for many years.'

'*We?*' said Lysander.

'Yes,' said Diokles, his eyes shifting like a lizard's on to Lysander's face. 'The *Krypteia.*'

The temperature seemed to fall in the room. *That's how Demaratos knew about Cato!* Lysander realised. His eyes caught the hilt of the dagger sheathed on Diokles' belt. Was that the weapon used to kill the young Helot man?

'Legend has it that after the war against the Messenians,' Diokles continued, 'a delegation once visited the great Oracle at Delphi, where the priests talk directly with the Gods. They asked the holy man how they could keep the Messenians under control. The Oracle told them a riddle: *Fear only the Fire of Ares.* At that time, no one knew this Fire of Ares was anything more than a legend. Like many of the Oracle's messages, it was difficult to understand. The Gods work in ways we cannot grasp.' He paused and hung the pendant back around his neck. 'But we are not taking any risks.'

Diokles reached the door and began to open it. Lysander noticed there was still some commotion outside, but he felt lost. *I can't let it end like this.* Feeling the swell of recklessness within him, he did the only thing possible.

'I'll fight you for it,' he said.

Diokles stopped, and turned.

'You will do what, *boy*?'

There was no going back.

'You heard me,' he said. 'The Fire of Ares belongs to me, and I will not let you take it.'

Diokles stood impassive at the doorway, and Lysander wondered what he would do next. Would he walk straight out, with the Fire of Ares? Or would he stay and fight – give Lysander one more chance? Diokles pushed the door closed with his foot. He interlaced his fingers.

'You know I cannot resist a challenge,' he said, cracking his knuckles. 'And I have not killed a Helot for a while.' He bent his knees into a crouch and held his arms out. 'When you are ready,' he said.

What in the Zeus's name have you done? Lysander asked himself.

What you had to do, a voice inside him answered.

As Diokles came forward, Lysander did his best to keep out of reach of his arms. If the bigger man got hold of him, it would be over. Every time Diokles came near, Lysander skipped away while trying to land blows on the outside of his tutor's arm. Every time

Lysander dodged his tutor's lunges, the more determined Diokles became, his arms swinging in wild arcs. Finally, Lysander found himself pushed back towards a corner of the room. There was nowhere to go.

Diokles swung a fist but the blow only glanced off Lysander's shoulder. Because of his bulk, the weight of the punch spun Diokles off-balance. This was Lysander's chance. He leapt on to the tutor's back, and wrapped his right arm tightly around his wide neck. Then he squeezed. Diokles' arms scrabbled to tear Lysander's strangling grip away, and then to claw at Lysander's face. He buried his head in Diokles' shoulder to keep his eyes out of the way, and with his other hand reached for the pendant. Once his hand wrapped around it, he felt immediately stronger.

The pair crashed around the room. *Surely someone can hear us*, thought Lysander. *They will come soon and put an end to this.* Beneath the din, he could hear the Spartan's wheezing breath, becoming shallower. Diokles was weakening in his grip, his hands becoming less frantic. *Just hold on*, Lysander told himself, *do not let go.*

Diokles threw himself backwards against the wall with all his weight. The mud-brick stayed firm, but a cloud of dust fell from the ceiling. Lysander felt the soft crack of a rib breaking, and had no choice but to let go. He fell to the floor among the pile of shields. Diokles keeled forward, landing on his knees and gasping for breath.

Lysander lay on his side, unable to stand, and looked

231

on in terror as Diokles rose to his feet. The eye patch had slipped down – there was nothing but a thin layer of scar tissue where the tutor's eye should be. Diokles readjusted the patch and rubbed his neck slowly with his hand. Lysander saw the tutor's fingers feel the empty space where the Fire of Ares had been. The pendant now sat snugly in his own fist.

'You nearly had me,' Diokles said. 'But it is over, Lysander. Give me the pendant.'

'No,' said Lysander. 'It belongs to me.'

'Then you can take it to the Underworld with you.' Diokles raised his foot above Lysander's head, ready to stamp.

Lysander knew that he was going to die.

He closed his eyes and waited.

CHAPTER 25

'Stop!'

The voice shattered the moment and a draught of cool air flooded the room.

'Stop! Please!'

Lysander dared to open his eyes. The tutor was frozen above him, and slowly lowered his foot. Lysander stared at the door of the hut.

'No, please, he has done nothing wrong,' Kassandra pleaded. But something was not right: she had her back to them. She was looking outside, towards the stadium and the sanctuary.

She was pushed roughly aside, and four Helots burst into the room. Two were carrying daggers, one held a javelin, a fourth had a wooden thresher from the field. It was old Nestor. Without hesitation, Nestor stepped forward and, swinging the farm tool, caught Diokles on the side of the jaw. The tutor's head snapped round with the force of the blow, and three teeth flew out of his mouth, rattling against the wall. His knees gave way and he dropped to the floor. Was he dead? No. A low, steady groan escaped the Spartan's lips. The javelin carrier came forward with a piece of twine, and manhandled Diokles' arms behind his back, tying his hands tightly together.

'Come on, you,' Nestor said to Lysander, pulling him from the floor. Lysander winced as pain stabbed where his rib had snapped.

'What is happening?' Lysander asked. The Helots did not reply, but it soon became clear when he stepped out of the hut.

The sanctuary had completely changed. Instead of the sounds of music, the night air was filled with angry shouting, screams of terror, pleas for mercy, and the occasional whimpering of fear. The neatly arranged tables were overturned and Helots rampaged through the Spartans on the hillside. All the slaves were carrying arms, some improvised from tools – sickles, plough handles, mattocks – others stolen from their Spartan masters. It was everything that Lysander had dreamt of for so long – a Helot uprising. Amid the chaos, he saw Kassandra a few paces away. Her fine dress was torn at the shoulder and three Helots pushed her between them, from one to the other. She could do nothing to stop them and the whites of her eyes glowed in the night. Lysander began to run over, the pain in his side shooting waves of nausea through his chest. He tripped on a rock and lost sight of them for a moment, his vision blurred. Then he saw that it wasn't a rock he had stumbled on, it was a body, tangled in a red cloak. A Spartan soldier, dead. As he struggled to regain his feet, he saw one of the Helots push Kassandra to the ground. All three laughed.

'No!' said Lysander, but his voice was weak. His head spun and his legs gave way again.

Lysander ground his fists against the earth. *Get up!* he commanded himself. Ahead, the laughing Helot who had pushed Kassandra suddenly spun round, the smile turning to a look of surprise. Lysander saw blood gush from his abdomen, and a figure launched in front of Kassandra. Demaratos. He held his injured arm to his chest. But in his other hand, Demaratus held a short sword dripping with blood. He lunged at the Helots, forcing them back. Lysander admired his bravery. But where there were two Helots, a third joined. Then a fourth. This was a one-against-many that Demaratos couldn't win. While he fended off one brawny Helot, another caught his legs with a piece of rope. Demaratos hit the ground, and a Helot kicked him hard in the side of the head. Demaratos lay still. The Helots seemed to have forgotten Kassandra now.

'Put him with the others,' said one, taking up Demaratos's sword. Two helots took hold of the Spartan's legs and dragged him away.

Kassandra brushed the dirt from her face, rushed over to Lysander and helped him to his feet.

'What can we do?' she asked, tears streaking her face, and her hair tangled with dirt. Lysander could not answer. Helots rushed from within the desecrated temple, carrying off sacred tripods and other objects. Many others carried torches and were setting them to the wooden structures nearby. As Lysander's eyes took in the pandemonium, there was a cry from the top of the slope where the spectators had been seated, and a wave of Helots flooded over the brow of the hill. This was no spontaneous rebellion – it was planned. Lysander watched helplessly as the Spartan men, women and children were rounded up into ragged groups and bound with rope. With most of the army still away, they were helpless. The atmosphere was deadly. Lysander caught sight of Timeon. He was grouped with some of the other Helots from the barracks, and they stood in a circle around a group of elderly Spartan men, armed with short flint daggers. His face shone with determination. Could he have known about the uprising all along?

'We have found Lysander!' shouted Nestor over the gathering. A cheer went up among the Helots. It was a sound Lysander had never heard before. His people were so used to being oppressed, they normally had little to cheer about. A pathway opened up among the crowd and Lysander was jostled along. Men clapped him on the back and blessed him. Lysander felt proud and powerful.

He stopped dead in his tracks when he saw the spectacle before the Temple of Ortheia. Kassandra's scream cut through the night.

In front of the altar knelt his grandfather, and above him stood a man in Helot dress. He was wearing the terracotta mask of the priest. Lysander knew this was sacrilege – a crime against the Gods. In the Helot's hand was the jewelled sacrificial knife used to kill the bull before the start of festivities. Sarpedon, with his arms bound tightly to his side, did not move or struggle – his cloak was ripped, his hair matted with sweat and blood, and his face emotionless like a granite carving. He had clearly put up a fight before they had over-powered him.

Sarpedon turned to Lysander, but he could not read his grandfather's expression. *Disappointment? Hope? Fear?* Lysander faced the Helot with the knife.

'What are you doing?' he asked.

'It is time to show the Spartans that we Helots are not their slaves any more,' came the deep, muffled voice from behind the mask. It sounded amplified in the stillness. 'We outnumber them ten to one, yet they treat us no better than beasts of burden. From this day, they will learn the folly of their ways.'

The crowd lifted a mighty cheer towards the stars and banged their weapons together. Once the clamour had died down, Lysander pointed to Sarpedon.

'And what are you planning with him?'

'This man is an Ephor of Amikles – the most powerful man in the town, and one of those who each year declares a war upon the Helots to keep us oppressed. Today his *war* will come back to haunt him. We will sacrifice him to the Gods as a blessing of our new freedom.'

The mob roared in delight, but Lysander heard a whimper behind him. Kassandra was being loosely held by Nestor, and her face was twisted with agony.

'Help him, please. Don't let them kill my grandfather.'

Lysander saw the faces of the Helots in the background. In the flickering torchlight, their expressions looked sinister. He understood then that he wanted no part in a massacre. He looked again at the would-be assassin.

'Killing these people is not the answer,' he said.

A laugh barked from behind the mask.

'And what do you know, half-breed?' The word shocked Lysander even more from the mouth of a Helot. 'You are one of them now. Of course you do not want us to succeed.' The crowd shouted their approval of his words.

'The rebellion will start like a fire. First here in Amikles, then the spark will catch across the five villages. We will burn Sparta to the ground! It's war!'

Another cheer. Lysander saw Sarpedon's head drop as torches were seized and new ones lit all around. He had to do something, and quickly. Then it hit him. *Of course!*

'Wait, all of you!' he shouted. He lifted his hand aloft, and let the pendant hang where all could see it.

'Behold, if you want fires and war, I have the Fire of Ares!'

It was as though a sudden wind had gusted from the stars. Some Helots staggered slightly. All were silent for several seconds. Then the muttering began. *Is it really the pendant? Is the prophecy true? How did the boy come to possess it?*

The masked figure must have been able to see the doubts setting in the hearts of the other Helots.

'It means nothing,' he yelled. 'The Fire of Ares is just a stone. Battles are not fought with jewels. We must fight with real weapons. This is our chance: here and now!'

Though the majority again shouted their agreement, the clamour was not as deafening as before.

'The Delphic Oracle itself has tied our destiny to the Fire of Ares,' countered Lysander. He looked from the bowed head of Sarpedon to the weeping Kassandra, her tangled hair hanging over her face. 'Cutting the throat of an old man, and murdering the defenceless is wrong!'

'Do not listen to him! What we are doing is the right thing! Tonight is our opportunity, before the bulk of the army returns. We must seize control now!'

Lysander made a show of studying the amulet closely, then showed it again to the Helots. 'It says here *The Fire of Ares shall inflame the righteous.* Ask yourselves, is this righteous? Look into your hearts. Look into the eyes of your prisoners. To kill in cold blood makes us no better than the worst Spartans.' The shadowy image

239

of Diokles and the other faceless members of the Krypteia came to his mind. *Their time will come*, he thought, *but not yet.*

Before him, Lysander saw the faces of the Helots crease in concern. They looked at each other in confusion. A few lowered their weapons. Lysander felt the advantage tipping in his favour.

'Let these prisoners go free. No Helot – no Messenian – victory has ever been won by spilling the blood of innocents. You have vanquished the Spartans today without shedding blood. This day will live on in their minds as the day the Helots spared them.'

Nestor spoke up.

'Maybe Lysander's right. We have all known enough of death in our lifetimes.'

Nestor was one of the most respected of his people, and this time several voices spoke out in tones of compromise. Lysander listened as the rippled murmurs gathered to a wave. One Helot walked forward and threw down his sickle. Another followed his example, dropping the short sword he must have taken from a Spartan, and soon Helots were dropping down their weapons all around. The two with daggers who had rescued Lysander from the hut stepped purposely forward and pushed the masked figure out of the way. But he was not ready to give up.

'You turned your back on your people,' he spat at Lysander. 'You are nothing but a traitor!' The words stung Lysander.

'He is not the traitor,' Sarpedon growled, twisting in his bonds. 'You are, hiding behind that mask. I know who you are. How could you betray me, after all this time?'

Lysander watched as the man dropped his sacrificial knife. A hand reached up and removed the mask. Strabo!

CHAPTER 26

Sarpedon's slave stared back, hatred lighting his eyes. He threw down the knife and ran in the direction of the fields. No one stood in his way. Lysander picked up the knife and cut through Sarpedon's bonds. Kassandra rushed out of Nestor's grasp and wrapped her arms around her grandfather's waist. Her body shook as she wept.

'But . . . I don't understand,' said Lysander.

'It is clear now,' growled Sarpedon, stroking Kassandra's hair. 'Who better to feed information to a rebellion than the slave of an Ephor? I cannot believe I was so foolish. I have known Strabo my whole life: he was my companion in the agoge, just like Timeon is yours. I trusted him completely – that is why I made him a free man. I thought he was staying with me out of loyalty, but I was wrong. He wanted information for the Resistance.'

Lysander sensed the crowd behind him grow restless again. They were not safe yet. He turned to address them.

'Listen!' he said. 'You showed yourself true heroes this evening. I have learnt a good deal in the Spartan school, but the lessons I carry closest to my heart are those I learnt as a Helot in the fields: bravery, perseverance, patience, and a sense of right and wrong. You have proved you have all of these qualities tonight.'

A lone voice spoke from the crowd: 'Yes, and we will be killed in our beds by the Krypteia for our sense of right and wrong,' he said sarcastically.

'That will not happen,' shouted Lysander, so everyone could hear. 'You have my word. One day our people will be truly free, but now is not the time. Go back to your homes and to your families, and bless the Gods that they are not without fathers, sons and brothers this evening.'

One by one, and then in groups, the Helots began to leave the sanctuary, peeling off into the darkness. As Lysander watched them leave, a hand was placed on his shoulder. It was Sarpedon.

'I am proud of you, Lysander,' he said. 'What you did tonight showed the courage of three hundred Spartans.'

While the spectators returned home and the boys headed back to their barracks or helped to tend to the injured, Lysander walked to the changing hut. He found Diokles where they'd left him in the corner of the room. The tutor was still unconscious. Standing over him with his sword, Lysander gazed at his throat. He lowered the point of his sword. No one would ever know it was him. *Diokles would kill me if he had the chance*, Lysander told himself. He steadied his aim. All it would take was a single thrust.

But no. He could not kill like this, like a member of the Krypteia. He leant down and sliced through the bonds that held Diokles' arms. The tutor grunted, but did not wake. Lysander slipped back out. Sarpedon was talking with a group of Spartan men by the Temple. Lysander headed to where Timeon stood with Orpheus and a tired-looking Leonidas. He caught sight of Kassandra. She had her back to him, and she was walking close by Demaratos away from the sanctuary. There would be time later to settle that score.

Thunder rumbled in the distance.

'We should get back,' said Orpheus. 'A storm is coming.'

Lysander glanced at the sky. A bank of blue-black clouds passed over the moon above. But it was the turmoil in Lysander's heart that preoccupied him. He looked at his companions in turn. *Do these people really know me?* he asked himself. *Do I know myself?* Tonight he had sided with the Spartans against his people. He had passed from being a boy to a man. But what type of man? Helot or Spartan?

'It has been a long night,' said Timeon from his side.

'It has, Timeon,' replied Lysander, as fat drops of rain began to splash on the ground. 'My mother always used to speak of destiny, of great events, but I never really believed her. But here we are – she was right.' He

244

paused and the rain fell harder. 'If I could wake up tomorrow and find today's trials washed away . . . but that will not happen, will it? This is just the beginning . . .' Lysander shook himself out of his reveries. 'Come on,' he said to his friend. 'Let's get back.' Who knew what tomorrow would bring? Whatever happened, the Gods would guide him. He would face whatever came with the courage of a warrior. As they walked back towards the barracks in silence, Lysander let his fingers rest around the cool stone that lay against his skin, back where it belonged. The words on the amulet burned like lightning behind his eyes: *The Fire of Ares shall inflame the righteous.*

Whatever Lysander had started, he would finish.